The
State of Chu

The Warring States Series – Book II

Greg Strandberg

Big Sky Words Press, Missoula

Big Sky Words

First paperback printing, 2015

Cover Artwork: Francisco Ruiz

Written in China

Printed in the United States of America

ISBN: 1514662213
ISBN-13: 978-1514662212

CONTENTS

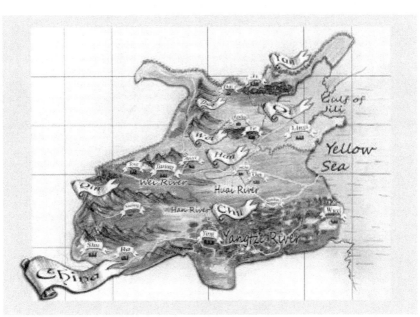

Map of China, c 400 BC

ONE

A blinding white light filled the sky. At nearly the same moment a deafening peal of thunder was heard. Sparks flew through the air and to the ground below as a large pine tree was struck and split completely down to its base.

"Run!" Wu yelled.

Wu jolted to his feet and pulled up Hai in the process. The two men bolted out from under the tree just as the large trunk split even further down the middle, the sound of the rain momentarily drowned out by the mighty tree splitting in two. They ran, but had chosen to do so in the wrong direction: that side of the tree was splitting off and beginning to fall, coming down right on top of them. Wu didn't have to glance back to know they wouldn't make it.

The sickening groan of the splitting trunk drowned out all other sounds as the two ran. The air started to rush up behind them and they could hear the tree falling faster. They both kept up their frantic pace, but it seemed to do no good. At the last moment, when the sound of the air was the loudest, Wu threw himself and Hai forward in a lunge, hoping to land clear of the tree. They were swatted like flies from the air by the heavy branches coming down and then pinned into the muddy ground as the tree came to rest on top of them.

Once again, the only sound was the falling rain, still coming down in torrents after more than three days. Wu gingerly opened his eyes and lay still for a moment. Heavy drops were smacking the mud around him. He didn't dare move, although he could already tell that nothing was broken. He lifted his face from the mud as much as the heavy branches would allow and turned his head to the side. Hai was lying next to him, and not moving.

"Hai!" Wu shouted above the rain. "Hai!"

Next to him Hai stirred and Wu let out a deep sigh of relief, the fear that had been growing inside of him checked. Hai tried to push himself up but the branches held him firmly.

"I can't move," he said.

"We've been pinned down," Wu replied, then swiveled his head to get a better look at their predicament. He could see that there were only a few feet of branches on either side of them, and a few more ahead. It looked like they'd managed to run most of the way out of the falling tree's path, far enough to at least avoid the thickest section of trunk and the heavier limbs. "I think that I might be able to crawl to the side and get up," he said after a few moments.

"Take your time," Hai said. "I think this is the driest I've been in days."

Wu inwardly chuckled to himself at his friend's words and took strength from his good humor. Despite all that'd happened to them in the past month, Hai still managed to retain his sunny outlook.

Wu slowly pulled his arms down to his sides and began to push himself up with his hands. Even though they were near the top of the tree the weight was still enough that he couldn't raise himself up. He pulled his arms back up ahead of him and clutched his hands tightly into the mud before pulling. His body moved forward a few inches, and he began to push with his feet as he pulled with his hands. He moved a few more inches and stopped, smiling to himself; even the forces of nature couldn't stop him for long.

After turning his body so that he was pointing toward the side of the tree, Wu again began to push and pull in the mud. It took several minutes, but he finally made it to the edge of the tree. Moving his arms back down to his sides he again pushed up, this time coming up enough to get one leg up then the other. After that it was easy to push the remaining branches away and stand up.

The rain immediately began to wash the grey mud from his light brown robes and he tilted his head back for it to do the same for his face, opening his mouth to take a drink and spit. His topknot had come undone and his long black hair was plastered all over his face. He took a moment to brush it away and looked back at where their small camp had been. Part of the mighty pine they'd chosen earlier that afternoon still stood, although it looked very strange with branches only sticking out to one side. A white streak ran down one side of the trunk, where it ended in a scorched and blackened mark on the ground. The other half of the tree lay on the ground, stretching nearly fifty yards from its base, and ending just a few yards from where he now stood. Wu shook his head when he saw how far they'd run in mere seconds. Shangdi certainly was smiling down on them this day.

Wu walked around the top of the tree to the other side and grabbed a few of the thicker branches and began pulling up. There was a scrabbling from under the tree and a few moments later Hai appeared from beneath the upraised branches. He rose up once he was clear and Wu let the branches drop. Hai glanced at Wu, then back at their camp, running his eyes back along the fallen tree before letting out a low whistle.

"We got lucky there."

Wu nodded. "Our first piece of luck in weeks."

"That's for sure," Hai replied.

Hai's hair was also in disarray, but he made no effort to remove the long strands from his face as he stared at the tree. He was younger than Wu, but not much, and age lines were beginning to show on his forehead and around his brown eyes. His light brown robes were as soaked and muddy as Wu's, but he seemed to not mind.

Wu turned and started to walk back to the half of the tree that was still standing, Hai falling in behind him. "Let's get our packs and be going," he said when they reached their small campsite.

"Lighting will never strike twice in one spot," Hai said behind him.

Wu looked up at the half-tree standing above them. "I'd rather not wait to find out."

Hai shrugged and began gathering the kettle and cups that lay around the now extinguished fire while Wu picked up their packs.

"It'll be dark soon," Hai said as Wu handed him his pack and he began tying the kettle to it.

Wu nodded. "I don't think we'll find another tree as dry as this one was, but we'll try."

Hai walked to the base of the tree and retrieved his sword. Despite the lightning having split the tree in two, his and Wu's swords were leaning against the side of the trunk still standing. He threw Wu his sword and then began to fasten his own to his waist.

"If we still had the horses we could have made it to the next town or village by now," Hai said as he tied his sword to his waist, some of the water from his soaked robes squeezing out as he fastened it tightly.

"Well, there's nothing we can do for that now," Wu replied as he finished securing his own sword.

Hai was about to reply when he caught a stern look from Wu. He held his tongue and slung his quiver of arrows over his shoulder instead, doing the same with his bow a moment later. He looked up again at Wu and nodded. Wu turned and headed back out into the rain.

They walked in silence through the forest, the only sound the rain around them. Their silences had grown more frequent over the past week since they had lost the horses. Two lone men traveling alone could be dangerous, especially when they were obviously not peasants, and especially in a state like Zhao. They had learned that the hard way, and now walked because of it. It was for that reason that they no longer traveled the roads, but kept to the forests and plains as much as possible.

Before, in the weeks after they had left the Wei Army camp outside of Xihe, Hai had spoken almost constantly, something that had grated on Wu at the time, but which he now realized the man had been doing only in an attempt to raise his spirits. Unfortunately the attempt had failed. Still, Wu was thankful for Hai's regard, for he realized now that he'd needed his spirits raised. He still couldn't believe he'd been relieved of command of his army, and then left the State of Wei for good. His decade's long service apparently meant nothing to the new Marquis of Wei, Marquis Wu, a man that Wu had been friends with in his younger years, and also a man that had grown to hate him over time. Wu shook his head to expel the thoughts and trudged on.

After several minutes of walking Hai called out behind him and pointed ahead with his hand.

"That looks like a good one there."

Wu followed Hai's arm to a tall tree with outstretched branches.

"Looks like there's even a few dry spots near the trunk," Hai added.

"It'll do," Wu said as he started forward again.

They walked the few yards to the tree, neither in a

rush, for they were both already soaked to the bone, and took off their packs when they got there.

"No use trying to build a fire again," Hai said. "I'll never find dry wood around here."

Wu nodded. "We still have plenty of bread and cheese."

Hai winced at the thought of another meal of the rock-hard bread and moldering cheese, but said nothing. In the next day, two at most, they would be out of the Zhao lands and could again travel the roads where inns were more frequent.

Wu took his pack off and sat down at the base of the tree before staring off into the distance. The General's despondency had grown over the past week since they had lost their horses, and Hai quickly took out some bread and cheese and passed it to his former commander.

"Another day or two and we'll be in Qi," he said jovially after Wu took the proffered food without comment. "Boy, they'll be glad to see you!"

Wu said nothing as he started in on the sparse meal, and Hai winced at his friend's demeanor. Wu had always been quiet, but never this quiet. It was becoming increasingly difficult for Hai to keep up the good cheer, especially when he had to force it, as was happening more and more.

"How long do you think it'll take for you to crush House Tian?" Hai said, pressing on despite Wu's mood. "Two weeks? Three at the most?"

Hai smiled his brightest smile but Wu didn't even look at him, just kept slowly chewing his food with that faraway look that Hai had come to recognize all too well. Unable to keep up the pretense of good cheer any longer, Hai lapsed into silence himself and the two men stared out at the rain around them while silently chewing their food.

TWO

"There it is at last!"

Hai pointed excitedly at the stone marker along the road that marked the border between the Qi and Zhao lands. Finally, after nearly two weeks of riding and walking, they had reached their goal of making it to the State of Qi.

Hai turned back to Wu, an eager look on his face, but Wu just gave the slightest of nods and walked by him. Undeterred, and his excitement undiminished, Hai rushed up to walk beside him.

"Now that we're in your home state I bet we could secure some horses rather easily," Hai said, beaming up at Wu. "With horses we could be in Linzi in a day or two."

"If we can get horses," Wu replied. "House Jiang only controls the capital and another small area, House Tian the rest; and I don't think that House Tian will be too eager to see me to the capital any time soon."

Hai's brow furrowed. "Surely House Tian doesn't control every horse trader in the state."

"I wouldn't be so sure of that," Wu said, "and I'm not sure if I want to find out. I think it's best if we stick to the smaller roads for awhile and just keep walking.

I'm known in Qi, and the last thing I want is for House Tian to know I've come back."

"I've never been in Qi before, so I'm not too familiar with the politics," Hai admitted.

"All you need to know is that House Tian and House Jiang have been fighting for the past hundred years," Wu explained. "House Jiang, which Duke Kang leads, has been steadily losing ground to House Tian during that whole time. Now they're barely holding on at all."

"That'll all change when you reach the capital, though, right?" Hai asked uncertainly.

"If I can meet with Duke Kang and he gives me men to command, yes," Wu said. "If for some reason he refuses my offer, then I don't see House Jiang lasting much longer."

Hai stopped and a moment later Wu turned back to look at him.

"It's that bad?"

Wu nodded. "It's that bad."

Wu began walking once again but Hai stood a moment longer with the puzzled expression on his face before rushing to catch up.

"Well, if that's the case, then-"

Wu suddenly raised his hand up, cutting off all further talk. He stood for a moment, then turned back to face Hai.

"Riders," he said. "In the distance, coming from across the border.

Hai's eyes grew larger. "Should we..."

"Just keep walking and act normal," Wu said.

Hai did as he was told, keeping a step behind Wu. After a few more moments the horses could be heard distinctly, coming up on the other side of the low rise that marked the border. After another few moments the first rider appeared, his dark purple robes dust stained from the road. Two more men came up behind him a moment later and all three slowed their horses to a walk as they spotted the two horseless men on the road.

Wu let out a sigh of relief when he saw from the men's robes: they were of House Jiang and not House Tian. Purple had always been the color worn by the rulers in Linzi, green the color favored by the rebels. Wu lengthened his pace, confident that the men would help him get to the capital that much faster.

"What are you two about?" the lead soldier called down, a grizzled man with few teeth showing in his mouth. Wu and Hai were within ten yards of the three riders, who were now completely stopped next to the border marker atop the rise in the road. "You're obviously not peasants, and from those swords at your belts I'd say that you're soldiers, deserters most likely."

"But from which army?" another of the soldiers asked, this one with a nose that'd been broken at least ten times. "Leaving Zhao, are they?"

"My name is Wu Qi, former general of the Wei Army in Xihe," Wu said confidently when he had gotten closer to the men. "I come to Qi seeking an audience with Duke Kang."

The three soldiers looked at one another then back at Wu. The toothless soldier, obviously in command of this small group, kicked his horse and circled around Wu and Hai, looking them both up and down before joining his two companions again.

"Former general," he said, a frown on his face, "why is that?"

Wu stared back at the man, his face revealing nothing. "After Marquis Wen died, his son, now Marquis Wu, deemed that my services were no longer necessary. I was dismissed from the Army."

"And now you've come here, back to your homeland," the broken-nosed soldier said. "What makes you think that we want you here?"

Wu narrowed his eyes at the man, but returned his gaze to Toothless. "I feel as though I would be a great help to Duke Kang in his fight against House Tian."

9

"How do we know this isn't some kind of trick?" the third soldier finally piped-up. This one seemed to share none of the sheer ugliness of the other two men, so Wu thought of him as Handsome; he'd learned long ago to name his enemies long before battle commenced.

"General Zhai Jue was supposed to help us against House Tian, but in the end he betrayed us," Handsome continued.

"And all of the other Wei soldiers have pulled out of Qi weeks ago," Broken Nose added, "along with those from Zhao and Han."

Toothless reached for the sword sheathed at his belt. "And now you come here, claiming to be the great Wu Qi. I don't believe you." He pulled the sword out and held the gleaming blade up in front of him. "I don't believe you for one second."

The man kicked his horse forward to cover the few yards separating him from Wu, but before his horse made it more than two steps an arrow suddenly sprouted from his chest. Wu saw the man's eyes open wide at the impact, and wider still when he looked down at the arrow sprouting from him. His horse made it a few more steps before he leaned over the side and then fell onto the road with a sickening thud. Toothless was no more.

Wu turned and rushed back the few feet to Hai, who was already nocking another arrow to his bow.

"Hai, no, wait!" he yelled.

"They'd have killed you," Hai said loudly as he drew the bow up to his face. He began aiming at the next soldier, Broken Nose, who was already racing toward them, his sword held high.

Hai loosed the arrow, but instead of striking the man in the chest as he'd aimed, it struck Broken Nose's left shoulder instead. The man grunted in pain, but his charge continued on.

Wu raised his sword up just in time to block the

first blow from Broken Nose's sword, bringing it up again to block Handsome's charge as the first man flew by him on the horse. Steel rang in the air as their swords met, and Wu hoped that Hai had dropped his bow and pulled his own sword.

Handsome continued to swing down at Wu, but Wu was quicker, and in between blocking the man's wild swings he thrust up with his own sword. One of his thrusts proved successful, piercing into the man's side. Handsome grunted in pain, but was able to swing down once more, although the attack didn't have the same force as the others, and Wu knew the man was finished. He thrust up again, piercing the same spot, then pulled his arm back to slash open the man's stomach. The man fell from his horse onto the road, but Wu was already turning back to Hai and the other soldier before he'd even hit the ground.

He was a moment too late. Ahead of him Broken Nose was pulling his sword from Hai's chest. Somehow the man had gotten off of his horse while Wu was engaged with the other soldier. Either he got knocked off by Hai or dismounted on his own. Either way, Wu realized, didn't really matter anymore.

Broken Nose glanced up at Wu and a smile spread onto his face when he met the General's eye. He pulled his sword up in front of him, the blood-stained blade taunting Wu. Wu clenched his sword tightly in his hand and moved toward the man at a slow but deliberate walk. Their swords rang in the air once, twice, and then again. The man was capable, but Wu had spent years training men in the finer points of swordsmanship, and this man had just killed his only friend and companion. Anger boiled inside him, but he kept it in check, using it to fuel his attacks. Fear crept into Broken Nose's eyes as Wu opened up with his full potential, increasing the frequency of his thrusts and swings, bringing down the man's defenses entirely. First Wu slashed across the man's left leg, then his left arm. A moment later two more slashes appeared on the opposite sides, the last causing the man's grip on his sword to falter. It was all that Wu needed: with a quick thrust he drove his sword into the man's chest, pulled it out, and turned away before the man was even sure of what had happened.

Wu was already at Hai's side when Broken Nose fell to the ground dead. He peered into his friend's eyes, but they just stared back at him vacantly. Wu squeezed his eyes shut and shook his head, silently cursing House Jiang and Qi. He came to help them, and this is how they repaid him, by attacking him and killing the only friend left to him. He opened his eyes and brought his hand up to close Hai's eyes, then stood up and looked at the scene around him. There were four dead men in the middle of the road, three of them House Jiang soldiers. The road was not a busy one, Wu knew, but it was still well-traveled. At any moment more soldiers could appear, and the last thing he wanted was to be accused of murdering his own countrymen. Still, he could not just leave Hai lying in the middle of the road, not after the man had left Xihe and traveled this far with him. They had been through too much together for that.

Wu moved over to one of the dead soldiers and wiped his sword clean on the man's purple robes before sheathing it in his belt. He then moved over to one of the horses and gently took its reins, smoothing down its mane as he did so. The animal was skittish, but didn't try to run from him. He led it over to Hai's body then reached up and unbuckled the saddle, letting it fall to the ground. He then bent over, lifted Hai's body, and threw it over the horse's back. *Well,* he thought sadly, *Hai finally had a horse again.*

The animal took a few steps back, and snorted its discontent. It didn't like the smell of blood, Wu knew, but he only wanted to ride a short distance until he was off the road and near some trees. Even a small stand would provide enough cover to bury Hai without anyone from the road noticing.

Satisfied that Hai's body was secure, Wu took the reins and led the animal over to one of the other horses and pulled himself up into the saddle, his robes bunching up about him. He took one last look at the three dead soldiers from House Jiang and shook his head before turning the horses back toward Zhao. As far as he was concerned Qi was dead to him. He kicked the horses into action and didn't look back.

THREE

"Your name?"

Wu stared down at the man in silence until he stopped writing and raised his eyes to look at Wu.

"Your name," he said with more insistence.

"Wu Li," Wu replied quickly.

"Wu Li," the man repeated as he made the brushstrokes onto the thin parchment, then moved down the page to write several more lines.

Wu stared off as the man wrote. After what had happened at the Qi border he didn't want to use his real name. Even this far south in Ying, the capital city of the State of Chu, he could be known. While he doubted that swords would be brandished in this small government office full of clerks and scribes, he knew that Chu Army soldiers were only a stone's throw away and could easily respond to a shout of recognition. He doubted that his name would elicit the same reaction as it had those many weeks ago along the Qi-Zhao border, though. Still, he wasn't about to find out.

"Qualifications?" the man asked, drawing Wu's eyes back.

"For more than ten years I've served in the bureaucracy of the State of Wei," Wu said, his words slightly true. "I started out at the bottom and worked my way up to quite an important position assisting their army."

The man leaned back in his chair. "Is that so?" His eyes bore into Wu as he brushed his long grey beard with his ink-blackened fingers. "If you had attained such an important position, then why did you leave?"

"Following the death of Marquis Wen there were...several shakeups to the army," Wu said slowly. "The bureaucracy was not immune, and my position was eliminated."

The man nodded, satisfied with the answer. If anyone knew the fickleness of bureaucracies it would be a pencil-pusher in Chu, Wu thought.

"You'll certainly not be going right up to an important position in Chu," the man said, once again resuming his writing. "In fact, you'll have to start at the bottom, like all new applicants. You'll be working with men half your age, and they won't think twice of stabbing you in the back on their rise to the top." The man stopped writing and looked up again at Wu. "But with if you work hard, and with your experience, I'm sure that you'll have a decent chance of advancing."

Wu nodded. Satisfied, the man continued his writing and after another minute came to the end of the paper. He made a few quick flourishes, stamped it, then turned the sheet around to face Wu.

"Seeing as you served with the army in Wei, that will probably be the best place for you in Chu."

"Oh, no," Wu said quickly, waving his hands in front of him. "If I have to start at the bottom I'd much rather try my hand at something new." The last thing that he wanted was a post in an army office where he might be recognized, but of course he couldn't say that.

The man frowned and turned the paper back around. "Well, in that case, why don't we put you into...oh, how about administration? It's the largest department of government, but advancement is still possible."

"That sounds fine," Wu said, relieved that the man hadn't asked more questions.

The man crossed out a few characters here and there, then again turned the paper around to face Wu.

"If you'll just put your name down here we'll be all set."

Wu took the brush and started to write his name. He paused, remembering that his name was now Wu Li, and wrote appropriately before turning the paper back.

"Well, that's it then," the man said with a bored look. "You're to report to administration tomorrow morning. Your duties will begin then."

Without another look the man put the paper onto a similar stack and reached for another. He quickly began writing once again, all thoughts of Wu forgotten.

Wu turned to leave. The busy office was full of men, both young and old, though mainly young, rushing about with stacks of parchment in their hands or quickly writing with brushes dipped in blank ink from small pots atop their desks. It was haphazard, and their seemed to be no purpose to any of it, but then Wu reminded himself that he was in Chu now, where the bureaucracy had become so bloated in the past fifty years that it was an entity unto itself, a living animal that pulsed and breathed with life, and which could just as quickly rise up and attack as sit at bay.

Wu made it to the door of the inner office and stepped out into the outer office, which was even worse. He managed to parry and dodge his way past clerks busily shuffling about and get out of the building unscathed. He turned back to look at the large stone structure, one of many in that area of the city, and frowned slightly. He hadn't anticipated spending his waning years shuffling papers in a government office, but he had little choice. He had left

Xihe in a hurry, both angered and humiliated by his loss of rank, and had taken little with him. Not that there was a great deal to take in the first place, but he had regretted his hasty departure several times over the days and weeks since then, especially when his small supply of money began to dwindle. The largest expenditure, and the main reason for his current lack of finances, had been the purchase of the two horses that lasted he and Hai for all of two days before they were confiscated by Zhao Army soldiers. Confiscated wasn't quite the right word; robbed would be more appropriate. Still, there were half-a-dozen of the soldiers, and while Hai had argued vociferously afterward that he and Wu could have easily dealt with the men, Wu hadn't been so confident that would have been the right decision. Dispatching them with their swords and bows would have been a simple manner; he doubted any of the six men had been well-trained, at least not as well as he and Hai. It was the worry that more could be a short distance away. The discovery of six of their own killed would have ensured a much larger force was sent out to deal with anyone found, whether guilty or not.

Wu shook off the thoughts as he turned away from the large stone structure and began walking down the cobbled street, careful to keep his eyes out for any gaps in the stones, of which there were many. Despite the large bureaucracy of Chu, they couldn't keep their streets properly paved.

Wu reached into his robes as he walked and bounced his money pouch in his hand. He could tell by the weight and by the sound of the coins that he was nearing the end of his rope. Within the pouch was barely enough money to secure even the poorest of lodgings and a few meals with it.

It had been much the same a few weeks before, when he had made the difficult decision to sell his sword. Down to his last few coins, he'd walked into a small town near the Wei River. The price he'd received was half of what he would have expected, and at least ten times less than the weapon was worth. But there was little he could do for it; he needed the money more than the steel.

The money lasted a few weeks, and he was soon down to only a few coins once again. It was that realization which brought him to the large government office in the first place; without a steady source of income he'd soon be living on the street like the countless other unfortunates he passed by on every street. They held out their dirty hands, most with at least one arm or leg missing, some blind, others diseased, begging for whatever handouts they could get. Wu had winced at the thought of sharing space with them during the night, so was left with only one choice: get a job. Thankfully, Chu was the one place in all of the Seven States where they were always willing to put men of intelligence to work, for their bureaucracy was endless, their need of skilled men capable of reading and writing great.

Wu turned onto another street and began walking down it. He was looking for the building that housed Administration, expecting it to be a large stone structure much as the previous Personnel building had been. Several stone buildings rose up on either side of the street, each with their names etched into the stone above their doors. There were numerous tax offices, army offices, education offices, foreign offices, and trade offices. Most of those buildings were large and Wu figured they conducted business for the whole state. Smaller stone buildings housed such disparate and seemingly redundant offices as Public Works, Street Maintenance, Poverty Control, and Pest Control. On just one block Wu saw different buildings devoted to weights and measures, one for fruits, one for vegetables, and yet another for grains. He suspected that they would also have one for meats, and perhaps another for tea. The sheer scale of uselessness and inefficiency of the Chu bureaucracy was plainly evident just by taking a stroll. And he didn't even want to guess at the amount of corruption needed to keep the wheels of it turning.

Another few blocks brought him to a large stone building that was as large as two other government buildings put together. Above its large double doorway rose a sign proclaiming it as Administration. Wu nodded, satisfied that he could find the immense building again. Now his attention could turn to finding suitable accommodations. He doubted that he had enough money in his pocket to get a room until he received his first month's pay. There was always hope that a proprietor of an inn would be understanding and allow him to stay, however. Wu wanted a place near the Administration building so he turned off onto one of the side streets that branched off from the larger avenue.

This street was in even worse shape than the one it came from, with more holes than cobbles showing. Obviously the Street Maintenance bureau wasn't doing its job.

Wu sidestepped holes, puddles, refuse, and beggars as best he could as he made his way down the street, all the while trying to keep his eyes up and scanning the numerous signs that hung down over shop doorways. Many were small stores specializing in stationary items such as pens and ink that would be needed on a daily basis by the large government bureaus surrounding them. Others were devoted to clothing, household items, and dry goods. By far the most numerous were taverns, and Wu figured that a great portion of the bureaucratic corps must spend their evenings here drinking away their wages. No wonder the system was so inefficient..

All of the taverns looked the same to him, and few of the signs said anything about being an inn as well as an establishment for food and drink. Still, judging from the windows of the buildings' second levels he suspected that many of them rented out rooms. Wu was nearing the end of the street, which was becoming increasingly narrow, and was about to turn around and head back to the main avenue to try another side street. Suddenly a sign caught his eye. *"The Barracks,"* it read simply. Wu hesitated a moment. A name like that would surely draw some of the military men of the city, yet the name called to him for specifically that reason. After a moment he shrugged aside his fears of being recognized and stepped toward the wooden door. It creaked loudly as he pushed it open, and it took him a few moments for his eyes to adjust to the darkness within.

"We'll not be opening up for lunch for another hour yet," a gruff voice called out to him from the back of the room.

Wu closed the door behind him. "Oh, I'm not here about food, at least not right now," he began, stepping further into the dark room. "I've come to inquire about a room."

Wu's eyes began to adjust to the darkness and the little amount of light able to penetrate the thin curtains of the windows. He could see a bar at the back of the large common room and stepped closer to it.

"A room, you say?" the gruff voice answered. "What do you be wanting a room here for?"

Wu could make the man out now, just behind the bar. He had short black hair which looked to have not seen a comb or brush in several weeks. His beard and mustache were thick and in an equal state of disarray. As Wu stepped up to the bar he could see that the man was old, in his late fifties at least, and that he had a deep scar running down one side of his face. Wu guessed that this man had served in the army, perhaps even seeing some combat during Chu's waning years of activity, and that he had opened this tavern as a way to supplement his meager pension.

"I'm to start work in the Administration building tomorrow," Wu said. "I'm new to the city don't have a place to stay. I thought that a place close to my work would be best."

The man looked him up and down for a moment, a frown coming to his face.

"And I suppose that you don't have the money to pay me now, either?"

Wu suspected that this man had seen countless young would-be bureaucrats come through his door over the years, asking for the same thing that Wu was now asking.

"I have some, but most likely not enough for a full month, at least until I'm paid.".

The man snorted, not at all surprised by the answer. "Figures," he said. "Well, how much do you have?"

Wu took the small money pouch from within his robes and upended it onto the bar. "What you see here is all I have to my name."

"Those are *bu*," the man said, his eyes shooting from the coins to Wu. "You come from up north."

Wu nodded. "I've been traveling through some of the others states."

"Well, we don't usually trade in *bu* here in Chu, just *yibi*, but if this is all you've got, then I guess it doesn't matter any longer."

"Will you take them?" Wu asked.

"I can change them easily enough," the man said after a moment, not mentioning that he would get a favorable exchange rate that would make the transaction quite worthwhile.

The man paused for a few moments longer and glanced from the small pile of coins to Wu. "A little old to be starting over again, aren't you?"

Wu shrugged. "I have no choice."

The man stared at Wu in an appraising manner for several moments before swiping the coins off of the bar and into his hand. He gave them another look then stuffed them into the pocket of his robes before coming around the bar.

"The room is this way," he said, moving toward the stairs.

Wu quickly followed and the two headed up the creaking stairs.

"The rent will be due on the first of each month, which is when you'll be paid. The price is ten *yibi* per month, and that includes your meals."

Wu nodded behind the man's back but said nothing. He wasn't sure exactly how much a *yibi* was worth in comparison to a *bu*, but he knew that ten *bu* was nearly an entire month's pay for a common soldier. He hoped that Chu bureaucrats made more.

They walked down the narrow hallway that ran the length of the building before the man stopped at a nondescript wooden door.

"This is the one," he said as he pushed the door open.

The man held his arm out for Wu to step inside. The room was little bigger than a common army tent, with the small bed pushed against one wall, a small table and chair taking up much of the other. A single window illuminated the room, which looked out onto another wooden building just a few feet away and across the narrow alley.

"There's a bowl for your washing and a pot for your other needs," the man said, stepping into the room behind Wu. "It's not large, but on your salary, you won't find much better."

Wu turned back to the man. "How much will I owe you at the beginning of the month?"

The man stared up at the ceiling for a moment before looking back at Wu. "With what you've given me, oh, I'd say three *yibi's*."

"Then I'll take it," Wu said.

The man reached into his pocket and pulled out a ring of keys, sorted through them, then selected and removed one.

"Lunch is served at noon, dinner at six," the man said as he handed the key to Wu. "I be Sa."

"Thank you, Sa," Wu said as he took the key.

The man nodded, gave Wu one more quick once over, then left the room, closing the door behind him. Wu turned and looked around again at the sparse room before sitting down on the bed. Well, he thought with a frown, time to start again.

FOUR

The chime sounded and Wu rose from his desk. He dipped his brush into a small cup of water then ran it over a cloth for a few moments, removing the black ink. He then laid it beside the ink pot, shuffled a few stacks of paper into one orderly pile, grabbed another stack, rose from his desk, and turned toward the door. The four other men Wu shared the small inner office with were each walking toward the door as well, nodding good night as they went. Wu was the last out and closed the door behind him, pulling a ring of keys from inside his robes to lock it. The large outer office was a bustle of activity as the younger clerks and scribes rushed about with stacks of papers. Each wanted to get to the right desks as quickly as possible so that they too could be out the building and on their way home, or more likely to their favorite drinking establishments. Wu easily moved through them and toward a side wall of the larger office where a man still sat at his desk. He looked up as Wu approached, a frown spreading onto his face.

"You just brought me a stack that size this time yesterday," the man complained.

"I know you like to keep busy," Wu said to the man as he laid the stack of papers down on the desk.

The man snorted but said nothing, not even glancing at the new stack that had just been added to the several already there.

Wu turned and headed for the door of the outer office, moved through to the long hallway branching off into yet more offices, and then through the front desk room before finally emerging from the building entirely. He didn't pause as he stepped onto the cobbled avenue and turned toward the small side street that led to his lodgings. He only noticed the numerous potholes as he stepped around them and didn't give the equally numerous beggars a look at all. Within minutes he was walking through the door of *The Barracks* and heading toward the bar.

Despite the fact that the final chime of the day had just sounded a few minutes earlier, the common room of *The Barracks* was already half-full. Men were busy throwing back glasses of wine and mugs of ale, the second already for many of them, Wu judged from the din of voices already growing loud.

Wu walked up to the bar but before he even reached it Sa had placed a small tray down with several bowls on it. Wu lifted one of the lids and steam wafted up into his face. Ah, beef tonight; Wu could tell from the smell. He put the lid back on the bowl, grabbed the tray, and headed for the small staircase at the side of the room. Another few moments brought him to his door, through it, and to the small table opposite his bed. He placed the tray down, pulled out the rickety chair, and sat down. A small brazier sat on one edge of the table and he picked up a flint and dagger beside it, struck a few sparks, and brought it burning to life. He lit a candle from the flame before extinguishing it, and then removed the lids from the three bowls, grabbed up his chopsticks, and started in on the rice. While he chewed that first mouthful he reached into his robes and pulled out his notebook, putting it onto the desk beside his tray. While still eating he took up his brush, removed the lid of his inkpot and dipped it in. With his other hand he opened the notebook to the marked page. After quickly scanning the text he put brush to paper and began writing with one hand while eating with the other.

Wu was still writing when a knock came at the door. He continued the line he was working on before leaning back in his chair. He could tell from the large puddle of candle wax on the desk and the darkness outside the window that he had been writing for several hours at least. He set his brush down, pushed himself away from the table, picked up the empty tray of food, and went to the door. Sa himself was standing in the hallway, his scarred face as usual betraying no indication of what he was thinking.

"First of the month today," the grizzled tavern-keeper said as Wu handed him the tray.

"Already?" Wu said with surprise as he reached into his robes.

Sa nodded resignedly but said nothing. After three years he had grown accustomed to the eccentric bureaucrat that lived upstairs. He seemed to have no need of friends, conversation, or companionship. In all the time Sa'd known him he'd only seen Wu come down to the common room for a drink a handful of times. And not once had he seen the man with a woman, or anyone for that matter. Still, the man paid his rent on time, although he usually had to be reminded that it was time, and he caused no trouble and made no noise. He was an ideal tenant, Sa had decided long ago, and he wished he could have more like him.

"Let's see, ten *yibi*," Wu said as he finally found his money pouch and began counting out coins.

Wu finished counting and handed them over.

"Not once in three years have you asked for a better room," Sa said as he took the coins and slipped them into his robe.

Wu's brows furrowed in puzzlement as he looked at Sa and then turned to look into the room behind him.

"Why would I want another room?" he asked.

Sa shrugged before he picked up the tray once again. "Suit yourself," he said as he walked off down the hall.

Wu knitted his brows and shrugged his shoulders as he watched Sa depart, then headed back into the room. He pulled another candle from a small box atop the shelf he had installed above the desk and lit it from the remains of the last, securing it upright in the still hot puddle of wax. The room now more fully lit, he grabbed his notebook and leaned back in his chair, scanning over what he had written that evening.

He flipped through the pages, paused on one, and began reading.

'...the amount of paper produced is in direct correlation to the amount of new personnel added to the bureaucratic offices. More people ensures that more paper needs to be produced. More paper produced ensures that more people need to be added to deal with it. More paper meant more people, more people meant more offices, and more offices meant more buildings. More buildings in turn meant that more people would be needed to build them. That will in turn lead to more paper..."

Wu stopped and closed his notebook, laying it on the desk. He leaned further back in his chair and looked up at the shelf above him. Next to the box of candles were all the notes he had written on the Chu bureaucracy over the past three years, neatly bound into two large leather-bound volumes. Wu stared up at them in admiration, for they were the only thing of consequence that had come about from his service to Chu during that whole time. The work he did in the Administration office was pointless, something he had realized after his first few days on the job. He had wanted to quit right then and there, heading back to

Qi to try once again to aid Duke Kang, or even to Anyi to plead with Marquis Wu to allow him that position training soldiers that he had turned down. He had quickly dismissed those notions, however, and persevered. After a few months he had even come to enjoy the monotonous paperwork that filled his days in the office, even if he saw no real use for it, and it was around that time that he began compiling notes on what he saw in the office. They were sporadically recorded at first, just a few observations about his superiors or coworkers, and written mainly on scraps of paper which he would toss away. After a few more months, however, he began to put some serious thought into compiling a detailed list of everything that was wrong with the Chu bureaucracy. Thought turned to action once he'd acquired the notebooks. That's when his role as administrator, a job he had willingly been looking forward to under Marquis Wen in Xihe truly came into being.

He kept his observations secret, only recording them at night in the confines of his own room, and he never spoke of them to anyone. He quickly came to realize that any talk of changing the bureaucracy was tantamount to treason in Chu, not so much because it was a great institution and desperately needed, but because so many knew how corrupt and inefficient it truly was. And, Wu had come to realize, the ones who held that opinion the most were the same men that served and often ruled over that corrupt and inefficient bureaucracy. Even though they knew of the futility of it all, they would not dare to change it. It was their work, their income, their rationale, their life. Without it they would be nothing, and without them, Chu would not know what to do. For fifty years the bureaucracy had stifled the once powerful state, making it a shell of its former self. Many knew this, but few wanted to admit it, even to themselves.

Wu closed his notebook and slipped it back into the

pocket of his robes. He reached his hand up and rubbed his temples and eyes. For some reason he was feeling a slight headache coming on. Perhaps it was reading over of what he had written. While writing he rarely thought much of what was being put down, the words simply coming to him in a torrent, his hand and brush often too slow to keep up. It was only when he chose to scan through the pages and even read a few that the enormity of the problem hit him, leaving him drained and feeling dejected. Wu rose from his chair, feeling just that, and looked over at his bed. It was still early, with several hours remaining before he usually went to sleep. He glanced out the window and down to the alley below, pondering whether to take a walk or not this evening.

The sounds from the busy common room below came up to him. Usually he had no problem drowning them out, rarely noticing them at all anymore, unless it was a particularly rowdy crowd or a fight broke out. It sounded as though neither was occurring tonight, however. Thinking that it had been some time, months perhaps, since he had last gone downstairs for a drink, Wu decided to do just that.

He left his room, closing and locking the door behind him, and went down the stairs to the common room. About two dozen men were scattered about the room, most sitting at wooden tables in the center of the room and against the walls. A few of the more inebriated men stood, speaking loudly on one topic or another to their particular group of friends or whoever was unfortunate enough to be within earshot. Wu took it all in and moved to the bar, where Sa was serving drinks and chatting with a few of the more regular customers and tenants that rented rooms.

"Well, this is a surprise," Sa said as he walked down to Wu. "What'll you have?"

"Wine," Wu said.

While Sa turned to retrieve a cup Wu turned and

leaned his back against the bar to better survey the room. Most of the men were young bureaucrats, although there were a few older men as well. He recognized one or two from his own office, although he didn't know there names. None seemed to recognize him, or if they did, they paid him no heed.

"Here you are, Wu," Sa said as he finished pouring the cup of wine. "That will be a tenth."

Wu fished out his money pouch and found the appropriate coin, a tenth of a *yibi*, and slid it across the bar to Sa. The inn-keeper slightly as he picked it up put it into the money box behind the bar.

"Got tired of writing?" Sa asked as he came back to the bar. The barkeep and owner of *The Barracks* had seen Wu writing at his desk many times over the three years that he had been staying there, most times after knocking on the door for several minutes without answer before opening the door to peer inside. Each time Wu had been so occupied with his writing that he hadn't noticed the sound, and a few times Sa had even mentioned that he had entered, retrieved the empty tray of food, and left the room again without Wu even noticing.

"I was beginning to feel a headache come one," Wu admitted.

Sa nodded. "I'm not surprised. You can't always stay cooped up in that small hole."

Wu didn't reply as he continued to look about the crowded room. Although most of the men were obviously bureaucrats, several seemed out of place. He turned back to Sa, who was moving further down the bar.

"Seems that the crowd is a little different that usual tonight," Wu said.

"Soldiers, and high-ranking ones at that," Sa answered as he came back. He looked past Wu at the men in the room. "I don't see him just now, but just a few minutes ago General Min himself was here."

Wu turned back to face Sa. "General Min? You can't be serious."

"Dead serious," Sa said with a stern look. "He sat right there, ordered dinner and drinks for his men."

Wu looked toward the table that Sa had nodded at and saw several men sitting about. He could clearly tell they were soldiers, his years in the army made that easy. None were in any type of military robes, however, and in fact their robes looked just the same as the bureaucrats that surrounded them.

"Where did the general go?" Wu asked, a feeling of nervousness coming to him.

"I'm not sure," Sa admitted. "Perhaps just to relive himself. I doubt he would have left his men."

Sa's attention was called away by a few thirsty men further down the bar and Wu picked up his own cup of wine, taking a deep drink of it as he stared at the table of soldiers. The last thing he wanted was for General Min to see him.

The two had met several years before. Wu had still been serving alongside Marquis Wen's son, Wu Wei, when they both were commanders in the Wei Army. They had been sent south to deal with a small clash of Wei citizens against citizens of Chu over grazing land. Two villages had eventually been pulled into the hostilities, both on either side of the border, so both states sent a small force to restore order. The citizens quickly fell into line when the two groups of soldiers appeared on the outskirts of their villages, and that same night the commanders of the two states had dined together before heading back to their respective capitals. One of those young commanders was General Min, and he and Wu Qi had spent a great deal of time talking about their two states' forces.

Wu knew that General Min would recognize him if he saw him, and that was the last thing he wanted. He had made it three years without his true identity becoming known, and he wanted to keep it that way.

Wu drained the last of his wine, set the cup down, and was just about to head for the stairs when the front door of the common room opened. General Min stood standing in the darkened doorway. He surveyed the scene before him for a moment before walking to his companions. Wu felt a wave of fear come over him; fear that he would be recognized and possibly killed. He was, after all, a former general of a rival state, and even though the peace agreement between the states had been in effect and observed by all for more than three years, there could be no certainty of how his situation would turn out if he were to be discovered

Wu hung his head and began walking to the stairs as quickly and as unobtrusively as possible. It was a short distance, with only a few tables blocking the way, and Wu felt confident that he could make it there and up to his room without detection. He glanced at General Min out of the corner of his eye and saw that he had reached the table of soldiers and picked up his cup of wine. He was beginning to say something to them in the same deep, loud voice that Wu remembered when suddenly Wu was covered in wetness.

"Oh! I'm dreadfully sorry," a young man said to him when Wu looked up. From the expression on the man's face, a slight smile curling the edges of his mouth, laughter tugging at his eyes, Wu could tell that he was anything but. The man, an obvious bureaucrat, glanced sideways at his companions sitting at a nearby table, each of whom was already beginning to break out in laughter.

"Please, let me buy you a drink to make up for it," the man quickly said before turning to yell toward the bar. "Sa! Sa! Get us another cup of wine over here!"

Wu, wine dripping from his head and face and onto his light brown robes to the floor below, turned back to the bar without thinking. Sa was staring over at him, as were many of the other patrons. Wu couldn't stop his eyes from jerking toward General Min's table, and he quickly regretted the action. General Min was staring straight at him, and their eyes met. It seemed like an eternity before Wu could pull his gaze away and turn back toward the stairs, pushing past the young man who was now laughing along with his friends. In fact, it wasn't an eternity but a single brief moment, but in that moment Wu had seen General Min's brows knit and his eyes narrow before they widened again. Wu knew that look: he had been recognized.

He walked as quickly as he could to the stairs and then, out of sight of the men in the common room, bounded up them two at a time. Wu was at his door in a flash, his keys already in his hand, and was soon inside. He didn't pause for a moment as he reached for the two leather bound books of notes on his shelves, stuffed them under his arm, and then turned for the door once again. Nothing else mattered to him, only the notes were important, although what he would do with them, and even why he was compiling them, was beyond him. He stepped out into the hallway and began to pull the door closed behind him, when he suddenly stopped. Even if he did want to escape, which he most assuredly did, he could not do so without going down into the common room. There were no other stairs, and the only back door of the establishment was through the kitchens behind the bar. Even if he had wanted to take that less obtrusive way out, he couldn't reach it without half the eyes of the common room going to him as soon as he came down the stairs.

Wu pushed the door back open and stepped inside. He looked around for a brief moment then rushed to the window. The drop down to the alley was less than twenty feet, and piles of refuse were heaped about beneath. Without hesitation he dropped his notebooks onto the bed and began pulling at the window, then, when it wouldn't budge, pushing. The window was sealed shut with years of grime, for Wu had never opened it before, and it proved nearly impossible to budge. Still, he kept at it, and after several moments the frame began to loosen from the grime it was encased in.

The stairs at the end of the hallway began to creak and Wu immediately stopped. The creaking came again, and Wu knew from the sound that someone was coming up. His eyes darted from side-to-side, panic beginning to edge in, and looked back at the window again. He would never get the thing open in time, His eyes fell upon the chair pushed under the table and without hesitation he reached for it. He had it over his shoulder and was just about to swing it at the window when a voice stopped him cold.

"General Wu, is that really necessary?"

Wu closed his eyes and let out a deep sigh, the chair still held over his shoulder. After three years of successfully staying unknown it all came crashing to an end with one spilled cup of wine. Wu lowered the chair back to the floor and slowly turned to face the man in the door.

General Min was a tall man, taller than Wu by a head, and would be forced to bend down if he wanted to enter the small room. His long black hair was tied in a neat topknot on his head, and allowed to flow down his back in a single long tail. His mouth was framed by a small, neatly trimmed beard and mustache while the rest of his face looked smooth and surprisingly young. His brown eyes stared at Wu with a mix of surprise and curiosity.

"You're not wearing your uniform," Wu said as he pushed the chair back to the table and motioned with his arm for Min to come in and sit down.

"I haven't worn that in some time, at least not in the capacity it was meant for," Min said as he ducked under the door frame and came into the room. "Once a year Duke Dao has some kind of elaborate ceremony in the palace and the uniform gets dusted off and worn for a night. Wine stains now take the place of the blood stains."

Wu waited for Min to sit down in the chair before sitting down on the bed opposite him.

"I seem to have found plenty of those this evening," Wu said, holding his robes out to look down upon the purple stains from the wine which had caused this meeting.

"And plenty of the other kind as well over the past few years," Min said. He leaned closer to Wu and spoke in a hushed voice. "I was sorry to hear about what happened to you when Marquis Wu came to power."

Wu nodded, a slight smile coming to the edge of his mouth. "Not as sorry as I was to experience it."

Min smiled before shaking his head. "He's a fool to dismiss his best general like that. What could he have been thinking?"

"About the past," Wu said quietly, then continued quickly as he saw Min's brows furrow in confusion. "But that was more than three years ago now, and, as you can see, I'm now quite content in Chu."

Min stared around at the small room before returning his gaze to Wu. "Living in a box like this and working in the Chu bureaucracy? I don't think so, Wu."

"I'm content," Wu replied.

"And it is contentment which filled those two books at your side," Min said, pointing at the two leather-bound notebooks still lying on the bed.

Wu instinctively moved his hand and pulled the books closer to him. "Just thoughts, they're nothing of any consequence."

"You're a terrible liar, Wu," Min said with a laugh. He smiled at Wu for several moments and then grew serious once again. "There is nothing to be afraid of,

Wu. No one in Chu means you any harm. There's no need for you to go by any other name but your own, and there is certainly no need for you to be working as a lowly clerk in the Department of Administration."

"How do you know these things?"

"I asked the barkeep who you were before coming up here," Min replied with a shrug. "He said you were Wu Li, had been living here for three years while working in the bureaucracy."

Wu shook his head. "It is no concern of yours what I call myself or where I choose to bide my time."

"Oh, but it is, Wu, it is." Min stared at Wu for several moments before continuing. "You see, Wu, you are one of the most capable generals in all of the Seven States. You would be a huge asset to Chu, or any state for that matter."

Wu shook his head. "My military days are over."

"Your talents as an administrator match those as a general."

Wu narrowed his eyes and knitted his brow. "What are you getting at?"

"Even if you *were* interested in joining the Chu Army, it would be a waste of your talents." Min threw up his arms and rose from the chair, causing Wu to lean back. "The bureaucracy stifles any attempt by the military to take action against even the weakest of the smaller states," Min said in frustration. "We cannot empty a chamber pot without filling out several forms, sending them off to the appropriate offices, and then waiting for a reply, which may or may not come. They've taken one of the most formidable armies in all the Seven States and turned it into a dog on a leash."

"Then why don't you do something about it?" Wu asked in consternation.

"I would if I could," Min replied, "but I can't." He peered out of the window as he continued to speak. "I'm an Army man, Wu, always have been. I know nothing about administering the lands that we

conquer; I leave those worries for others to argue over."
He turned back to Wu, a glimmer in his eye. "But you,
Wu, you know all about those sorts of things."

Wu shook his head. "You're confusing me for
someone else, Min."

"No, I'm not," Min said as he again sat down in the
chair, this time leaning in to talk to Wu. "All of the
other states were abuzz with what you were doing in
Xihe over those five years that you fought there. We've
never seen changes the likes of which were made
there, Wu. You not only took the lands under your
control, but you kept them by the demand of their own
people. Those policies continue to be talked about in
all of the Seven States. I could never have made those
changes; no one I know of could."

Wu waved his hand dismissively. "That's all history.
Others are governing Xihe now, not I."

"And they're not doing half the job that you did,"
Min said.

"I don't understand what that has to do with me
now."

Min leaned back in his chair and studied Wu for a
few moments. "Duke Dao is ready to take on the
nobles and gut the bureaucracy."

"I've heard that talk before," Wu said.

"It's for real this time, Wu. He means to make some
serious changes before the year is up."

"Impossible, the bureaucracy is too large, the nobles
too controlling. They'd stop any attempts before he
even got started."

"Not if the great General Wu Qi was overseeing the
changes," Min said.

Wu laughed. "You're dreaming, Min."

"Am I?" Min rose from his chair and sat down on
the bed beside Wu. "I'm heading straight to the palace
to tell Duke Dao that you're here, whether you like it
or not."

Wu shook his head. "Please don't do that, Min. Let

me continue on as I have."

"That I cannot do, Wu. It would be an injustice to not only you, but to Chu as well."

"I'll leave."

Min let out a sigh. "We'll find you, Wu. Now that we know you're here, we'll find you."

Wu stared at the floor but said nothing. His world was suddenly crashing down around him, and there was nothing he could do to stop it. The carefully prepared life that he'd created for himself was no more. Wu Li was gone forever, changed back in an instant to Wu Qi.

Min rose from the bed and stared down at Wu. "Come with me, Wu. Meet with Duke Dao." Min pointed at the two books still sitting next to Wu. "Tell him of your thoughts on the bureaucracy. Show him your books."

"The nobles are too strong, the bureaucracy too large," Wu said quietly and without conviction.

"Tell him how to change that, Wu."

Wu looked up at Min, sorrow in his eyes. Min gave smile in return and held out his hand.

Wu looked at it then down to the floor. *What do I have to lose*, he thought. He looked back up at and grasped the general's hand.

"You've made the right decision," Min said as he helped him to his feet.

"I'm not so sure of that," Wu replied.

"Perhaps not now, but you'll come to see the wisdom of it with time."

Wu reached down and again picked up his books and put them under his arm. Min stepped back out into the hallway as Wu took one last look around his small room. He blew out the candle, plunging the room into darkness, and then stepped out into the hallway beside Min, pulling the door closed behind him.

FIVE

Even in the dark of night the Chu Royal Palace reared up resplendently from the otherwise dull and barbaric structures that crowded around it. The palace, much like the rest of the city, was a constant work in progress: it was continually in the process of either moving out or moving up, and sometimes both at the same time. Unfortunately, as that movement took place the quality and beauty decreased markedly. Although the palace was quite resplendent as Wu and Min approached it, its outer face was nothing compared to its inner.

The Palace grounds were surrounded by a low wall which rose up behind a moat that had long ago ceased to hold water. The two men walked over the wooden bridge that spanned the dry and cracked stone beneath them and then right past the two sentries manning the gate, both of whom gave a deferential nod to Min. Once inside the wall, the appearance of the palace grounds became better, although it was nothing compared to the palace in Anyi, Wu thought. All throughout the stones of the buildings and walls were cracking from neglect and improper construction. Weeds sprouted from the bricks at their feet and refuse was piled about haphazardly. Still, it was cleaner and more maintained than much the city, although Wu couldn't quite decide if that was good or bad.

Entering the palace itself proved just as easy and they were soon walking down the carpeted halls. Tapestries depicting Chu's military achievements over the previous centuries lined the walls, each showing a victory over large and small states alike, although Wu knew that most had been small. At last they came to a door that had several guards and Min had to stop and request an audience with Duke Dao. One of the guards nodded and slipped through the door.

"Is it common for you to come to the palace at night like this?" Wu asked while they waited.

Min shook his head. "I haven't been to the palace in nearly a year."

Wu's brows furrowed in surprise. "You can just enter any time you like?"

"I'm Duke Dao's leading general," Min answered. "If there's something that I need to tell him then I'm to come to him directly."

Wu nodded. At least there was one small part of Chu that wasn't weighed down by the bureaucratic slowness that so plagued other areas of the government; usually any type of action took days, if not weeks or months.

After a few minutes the guard returned through the door, holding it open and indicating with his other arm for the two men to enter. They walked down another short hallway which ended at another set of double doors and yet another two guards. The door was opened for them and they stepped through into a large room that was dominated by a huge wooden desk. Seated at it was Duke Dao, his long grey hair flowing down his back, his bushy grey eyebrows nearly covering his piercing brown eyes. He rose when the two men entered.

"General Min, it's good to see you again," he said

with a smile. "I hope that everything regarding the army is sound and that this is just a social visit." He glanced at Wu when he said the last, but Wu couldn't tell if the Duke recognized him or not.

"There are no troubles which require the army's services, if that is what you mean," Min said coolly, "but the other problems which the country faces, and which I've spoken to you at length of in the past, are still plentiful."

"Yes," Dao said as he sat back in his chair, "the other problems." He stared hard at Wu for a few moments, looking him up and down, as if deciding if the man now standing next to his leading general were a friend or an enemy. The distinction most likely rested on what Wu said.

Min raised his hand up and indicated Wu. "Tonight while dining at an inn near the Administration Department I happened upon General Wu Qi. As you know, Sire, Wu Qi was the leading general in the Wei Army until Marquis Wen's death. When Marquis Wu came to power he, for reasons beyond me, relieved Wu of his position at the head of the army. It was Wu Qi who led that army in taking the Xihe area from Qin. He was just beginning to oversee administratively when he was relieved of command."

"Yes, I thought that you looked familiar," Dao said as he continued to look at Wu. "So tell me, Wu Qi, what is it that you are doing in Chu?"

Wu cleared his throat and gave a deferential nod to Dao. "Sire," he began, the title feeling out of place on one who was not Marquis Wen, "for the past three years I've been working as a clerk in the Administration Department."

"A clerk!" Dao cried out loudly before laughing a short, sharp laugh. "Why, whatever for?"

"When I was dismissed from the Wei Army I had very little," Wu explained. "I traveled a bit, eventually making my way here to Ying. By that time I was nearly out of money and needed a job."

Dao knitted his brows. "Why have you stayed so long? Surely you would have wanted to go back to your homeland, the State of Qi?"

"I had planned to, and did cross the border from Zhao into Qi shortly after leaving Wei." Wu frowned slightly at the memory of that day's attack. "I had wanted to aid Duke Kang and House Jiang against House Tian, but it seems that I was not wanted there."

"Not wanted?" Dao laughed again. "Kang is even crazier than I thought."

Wu lowered his head and looked at the floor for a moment while Dao regained his composure and stared at Wu once again.

"So you've been working in our bureaucracy for three years, eh? Well, what do you think?"

"I'm happy for the opportunity to work there, and I-"

"I'm not interested in whether you like it or not," Dao interrupted. "I want to know what you think of it."

Wu looked up at Dao, his eyes narrowing. Dao sensed the dangerous look and sat up straighter in his chair.

"Well?" he said, peering back at Wu challengingly.

"It's like a large snake that has coiled itself around Chu, squeezing the life out of it with each breath," Wu said levelly.

"I see," Dao said, a bit taken back by such a blunt statement. "And I suppose that in your three years as a clerk in Administration you've come up with the solution for such a problem."

Wu nodded. "The snake, and all those feeding it, must be killed."

Dao's eyebrows rose at the remark and he leaned back in his chair. He stared at Wu for several moments as he stroked his pointed grey beard, then looked to Min.

"I've heard such pronouncements before, Min. Why

is this man so special?"

"Sire," Min began, "Wu has compiled several notebooks worth of material on the problems the bureaucracy faces." He pointed down at the leather notebooks that Wu still held clutched under his arm. "Furthermore, he is one of the most able administrators in all of the Seven States. The changes that he brought to the conquered Xihe lands not only stopped any aggression against the Wei Army while they pushed further west, but made those lands more productive and more profitable. And all the while the attitude of the people was changed from hostility to admiration."

"You speak very highly of him," Dao said.

"I do, Sire, but only because he has earned such high praise."

"And what changes would you make, Wu Qi?" Dao asked as he turned his gaze back to Wu.

Wu took the two notebooks out from under his arm and motioned with his head toward the table. Dao nodded and Wu moved forward, laying one of the books off to the side of the table while opening the other. Both Min and Dao leaned in to see what secretes the book held.

Wu flipped through a few pages of neat, handwritten notes before settling on what looked to be a list.

"The government of Chu has become corrupt and inefficient largely due to the greed of the corrupt and inefficient bureaucracy," Wu began, looking straight at Dao. "There are a number of reasons why this has come about over the years, but they aren't important for the solution. There are a number of changes that need to come about to correct the situation and return Chu to the glory that it once knew."

He paused to look over at Min and again at Dao.

"Go on," Dao said, his curiosity piqued by what the former general had to say.

Wu nodded and pointed down at the list on the

page. "The annual pay of all officials, regardless of position, must be lowered. Furthermore, the corrupt, inefficient, and just plain useless among them must be dismissed."

Dao gave a low whistle. "That's a tall order."

Wu nodded. "It only gets taller." He again indicated the list on the page. "The hereditary privileges enjoyed by the nobility for the last three generations must be eliminated."

"Now see here," Dao said angrily, "those privileges were put in place for a reason! They cannot just be taken away."

"The reason for those privileges was to win the support of the leaders of the smaller states that Chu conquered," Wu said. "What was once meant to cement good relations has now become a drain on not only the treasury but the effectiveness of Chu's ability to function."

Dao put his hand on his hips and was about to argue further when Min raised up his hand.

"Sire, please, let us hear what he has to say."

Dao stared at Min angrily but after a moment frowned and nodded his head.

"Continue," he said through clenched teeth.

"The money that's saved from lowering the pay of the officials, as well as cutting more than half of the bureaucratic positions, together with that kept here in the palace's treasury and not that of the nobles', will allow Chu to train a more efficient and professional army."

It was Min's turn to look at Wu in wonder tinged with anger. "You're saying that the army is neither of those things now?"

Wu nodded. "Chu still equips and trains its army like it has for the past hundred years. Nobles no longer comprise the majority of the army ranks in the other Seven States. That has changed some time ago. Civilians are now forming the majority of both the regular soldiers and the commanding officers."

"To take away both the hereditary privileges of the nobles as well as their standing in the army is quite a blow," Dao said. "I don't think it can be done."

"That's a choice that you'll have to decide upon yourself," Wu said. "I can't do it for you."

Dao stared at him for a moment before looking down at the opened book. "Is that all?"

"No," Wu said with a shake of his head as he put his finger down on the next item in the list. "High-ranking officials in the bureaucracy and the nobility must be moved away from the capital and to the borders."

"Whatever for?" Dao asked, more perplexed than angered by this last statement.

"It will reduce their power over the throne as well as taking their talent to areas that need it. They can be put to use making those areas of the state more productive, which will in turn encourage more people to settle there."

"I'm not sure that a lot of people would feel comfortable settling along the border with Yue," Min said as he folded his arms across his chest.

"They will if the leading nobles of the country show them the way," Wu said.

"Perhaps," Min answered after a moment of tugging on his short beard.

"I see one more item on your list, Wu," Dao said. "Something about buildings, it looks like."

"Correct. A new set of building codes must be instituted to make the cities look less barbaric."

Dao threw up his hand and turned away from the table. "The other changes I can listen to and see some sense in," he said in frustration, a smile of unbelief on his face, "but this last is beyond me."

"I've seen better buildings among the Rong Tribes to the north," Wu said. "Even though their position on the border of the Seven States is a precarious one at best, they build to last. That isn't something I see in

Chu." He paused, waiting for both men's full attention. "Even walking through the palace grounds tonight I was struck by how poorly the palace itself is constructed. Stones are cracking and crumbling as weeds sprout from the sides of walls. It certainly isn't a sight to inspire confidence in the people, or awe in your enemies. The first things that a visitor to a new city sees are the buildings around him. If they rise up majestically and beautifully he is awed and impressed by the will and power of the state. If they stare back at him dejectedly and in disrepair he feels nothing but disrespect toward a people that would allow such poor construction to occur. And when he returns back home to his own state his scornful opinions will spread. All respect for that state is gone."

"I see," Dao said a few moments after when Wu had finished.

Wu closed the book and stacked it on top of the other. "Those are the most pressing problems, as I see them, and the ones that must be dealt with immediately if Chu is to regain its former position as one of the leading Seven States." He picked up the two books and put them back under his arm before turning away from the table and heading toward the large double doors. He paused halfway there and turned back. "You might think that these changes could never be carried out, but I assure you they can and they must. If serious changes like those I've mentioned here tonight are not instituted then in a generation, perhaps less, Chu will be as weak as Qin. And in another after that it'll be nothing more than a small state with the ego of a large." Both Dao and Min stared back at him but said nothing. Wu just shook his head.

"Now, General Min, Duke Dao, if you will please excuse me, I have to report early to the Administration Department in the morning and I need my sleep." He gave a low bow before turning back toward the doors.

Duke Dao and General Min just stared and said nothing as he left the room.

SIX

"We can be pushed no further!" Pai Fen roared.

A raucous applause greeted his words, and Pai Fen stood stoically in the center of the crowded hall until the cheering died down. His long, grey hair was tucked neatly under his dark red hat while his long beard and mustache flowed down into his matching dark red robes.

"Already we've had our hereditary privileges stripped away from us and our annual pay lowered, all the while watching several of our fellows forcibly moved to the borderlands," Pai yelled out in his deep, booming voice before the cheering had died down completely. "I tell you again, we can be pushed no further!"

The hall again erupted in applause, this time with several men near Pai rising to show their support. They were quickly followed by others behind them and to the sides. Within moments all of the assembled nobles of the Noble's Council were on their feet, clapping loudly at the words that Pai had said, and for his willingness to say them.

Pai gave a nod and slight bow before moving off of the open floor and back to his seat, the men around him clapping him on the back and offering encouraging words. Pai nodded to them again and sat down, the others in the hall following his lead. The hall quieted down and after a few moments another man rose across the open floor from Pai and strode out.

The hall grew silent as Dao An stopped in the center of the circular marble floor and stared out at the assembled nobles. His head was clean shaven and shined in the light of the sun from the gallery windows as well as the torches burning on the walls. His long black mustache and thin beard spilled down to his chest, although, judging from the lines around his eyes and the wrinkles of his face, most suspected that he dyed them regularly. His dark green robes seemed to swallow up his thin frame as he inwardly frowned at the sight before him: the hall, meant to hold three hundred and which had done so easily over the years, often overflowing into the hallways without, was now peopled by less than one hundred men. He shook his head, causing a few murmurings from the seated men.

"Over the years Pai Fen and I have rarely agreed on the issues before us" Dao began in a soft voice that even those nearest craned their necks to hear, "but on this issue before us today, perhaps the most important which has come before us in all our years of service, I can do nothing but agree with him."

A few men in the gallery clapped and several others began speaking in hushed voices, but others around them quickly quieted them down; no one wanted to miss what Dao had to say.

"To say that the changes that have been implemented over the past two years have been anything less than earth shattering would be an understatement," Dao said in the same quiet voice. "Never before in the history of Chu has their been such upheaval among the nobility while the rest of the country remains unaffected. Not even in times of war," he pressed on, his voice rising in pitch and tempo, "have such drastic changes been made. I ask you men, are we at war?"

"No!" many of the men in the gallery shouted down to him.

"No?" Dao said with furrowed brows, causing the men that had just shouted so forcefully to suddenly look unsure of themselves.

Dao raised his arms up to the men around him, his voice becoming more forceful. "Is it not war, I ask you, when all that we have been promised for generations is taken away from us?"

Several of the men in the gallery nodded their heads and looked at one another for support.

"Is it not war when money that has gone to us for years, money that is paid for our tireless service and heartfelt devotion to the State, is suddenly taken away and instead given to the peasants who now call themselves soldiers?"

More men nodded, a few even yelling out in agreement at Dao's words.

"Is it not war when hundreds of our peers are told in the dead of night that they must pack up what belongings they can, that they are being moved away from the only city they've ever known, to spend the rest of their days in some dusty town? And for no other reason than that a general from the State of Wei thinks it's a good idea?"

"It is war!" one man shouted from higher up in the seats, and several men jumped to their feet to voice their agreement.

Pai Fen stared at Dao An with a smile on his face. The man had always known how to get the crowd in the palm of his hand, and he was doing just that here today. What most surprised Pai, however, was that he was smiling. Usually when Dao got started, he was arguing against Pai. For once, and for the first time that Pai could remember, they were both on the same side.

"If it is war," Dao said, his voice now loud enough

for people outside of the hall to hear, "then the question is, 'what are we going to do about it?'" He peered questioningly at the men around him, his eyebrows raised in anticipation. "Will we just sit back and let it happen? Will we just sit back and do nothing until all that our forebears have worked so hard to attain is taken away from us bit by bit until we have nothing left?" Dao paused, his head cocked to one side, his eyebrows arched, the hall on edge. "Will we just wait until we are nothing more than common peasants?"

The hall erupted in angry cheers as men all around the gallery shouted out that they would not just sit back and let those things happen to them. Dao gave a slight bow and moved off the floor and back toward his seat, receiving the same good cheer that Pai had received before him.

The crowd was still restless and on their feet when the next man rose and strode out onto the floor. Fei Lin could not have been any more different from the two men that preceded him. Whereas both Pai and Dao wore richly-made robes and took great pains with their hair, Fei eschewed such extravagances in favor of the simple brown robes worn by the majority of the peasants. His long black hair was tied in a simple queue down his back and his face clean-shaven. The hall quieted down as he stepped onto the center of the floor, although there were quite a fair amount of stifled laughs and mocking words for him. Fei Lin couldn't command the same respect as his better-known and well-liked peers, both of whom were from rich and prestigious families that could trace their lineage back for a thousand years. But as the leading Daoist of Chu, he was afforded a certain amount of respect, although it came grudgingly at times.

"Pai Fen says that we will not be pushed any further, and Dao An says that we are at war," Fei began in a loud voice so that he could be heard over the hum of voices. "But what I ask you is this: how are we to stop those changes from happening and how are we to win this war that we suddenly find ourselves in?"

He stared out at the gallery of men, but no one called out an answer to his question.

"I'll tell you'll how we'll stop it," Fei said, pausing to make sure he had each man's attention, "by doing nothing."

The gallery erupted in murmurs as men talked to themselves and shook their heads at what Fei was saying. Fei held up his arms to silence them, which he managed after a few moments.

"The history of Chu has been a history of war," Fei said, "and once again Chu is heading toward war. Sure," he said with a glance and a raised hand toward both Pai and Dao, "some of you think that that war is being fought against us, the nobles, but I assure you, it is not. It is being fought against the slothful nature that Chu has found itself mired in for these past fifty years. That proud military tradition which many of you so fondly reminisce on, and which I have spoken out against more times than I can remember, is once again coming back to Chu. And it is coming, gentlemen, not at the urging of those of you gathered here today that spoke so lovingly about it, and yearned for its return, but by a disgraced general from another state who, just two years ago, was a lowly clerk in some lowly government office."

Several of the men in the gallery began nodding at Fei's words, and they emboldened him to continue.

"As we speak, the money that was taken from us and from countless other government officials is being used to grow a larger, better-trained, and more powerful army. The commanders of this army, our beloved General Min being the foremost among them, are already planning a campaign against the State of Yue, a State which only grew to such heights of power through our support. Unfortunately, we cannot control or even hope of defeating Yue because of our own corruption and inefficiencies.

"I tell you, we will change what many of you feel are injustices being perpetrated against you not by shouting out our disproval and vowing to go to war with the throne, but by doing nothing, by waiting, and letting the plans that have been carefully laid take their course. When our army completes its task against the State of Yue, then all will return to normal."

"And if it doesn't?" a voice called out somewhere from the gallery above.

"And if it doesn't, then perhaps that would be the time to listen to the more...forceful plans that we heard here today."

Fei waited a few more moments before bowing slightly and walking back to his seat, receiving neither the applause nor the claps on the back that his two peers received after their speeches.

Pai Fen rose from his seat and raised his arms to draw the hall's attention.

"Gentlemen," he began. "We've discussed much here today, and time is needed to allow those thoughts and ideas to settle in our minds. Let us adjourn for the day."

Nearly all of the men in the gallery rose from their seats before the last words were out of Pai's mouth. Pai turned and clapped a few men on the back while shaking the hands of others, assuring each that he would give another speech saying much the same thing when the Council next met. After a few moments a hand fell on his shoulder and he turned to thank yet another man, but stopped when he saw who it was, his eyes widening and his brows rising.

"I never thought that I'd see the day that we agree on an issue," Dao said, his dark eyes narrowed from the lines around them.

"Nor I," Pai admitted as he put his own hand on Dao's shoulder, "nor I."

"Now if we would have had Fei on the same page as us, well, then I think that I would have dropped dead from surprise," Dao chuckled.

Pai smiled. "Trying to discern where his sympathies lie is like trying to divine the truth from a blind hag of a seer: costly, time-consuming, and not at all worth the effort."

"And once divined you'll find that the opinion has changed to the opposite the next day," Dao said.

Pai laughed and clapped Dao on the back, turning him so that they were standing side-by-side.

"I for one will not be wasting my time trying to discern that one's views," Pai said. "It would be a waste of my time. No one cares much for what he has to say anyway."

"But he does have support," Dao said. "You don't become the most powerful Daoist in Chu, and one of the leading Daoists in all of the Seven States, without friends."

"True enough," Pai said, "but did you truly come over to me to speak about Fei?'

Dao stopped and turned to face Pai. "No, I did not. I came because I hoped that we could speak in private."

Pai's eyes narrowed. "About agreeing more often?"

Dao shook his head. "About the troubles that are plaguing us, and about a certain outcast general in particular."

Pai nodded. "For that I am all ears."

"That's what I was hoping to hear," Dao said as he turned and began walking with Pai once again.

SEVEN

General Min opened the door and was immediately assaulted by the noxious odors of both wood and kitchen smoke, neither of which was afforded much of a chance to escape the stuffy common room with its windows and doors closed tight. He waved his arm in front of his face in an attempt to disperse some of the cloud that engulfed him upon entering. It was a futile gesture and Min was forced to move slowly through the haze toward the bar.

"Min," a voice called out to him from somewhere to his left. He stopped and turned in that direction, narrowing his eyes to get a better look. He widened them a moment later when he saw Wu Qi sitting at one of the tables near the far wall, and started toward him.

"You're early," Wu said when Min reached the table. "I didn't expect you so soon."

"Duke Dao was not in the palace but out viewing the troops," Min said as he pulled out the chair across the table from Wu and sat down.

"He's been doing that quite often these days.

Min nodded. "That he has. Ever since the first time he rode out to take a look at what your changes had wrought in the army. He's come to realize that the

Chu Army of yesteryear is once again coming together."

"All I hear him talking about when I meet with him is how Yue will be crushed underfoot when the army is ready," Wu said as he raised his arm and waved toward the bar.

"That's still some time away," Min said with a frown, his eyes on the table.

"Not the way I'm hearing it."

Min was about to argue against whatever it was that Wu had heard when the barkeep appeared at the table.

"Sa, bring another pot of tea and a cup for General Min," Wu said, then glanced over at Min. "Unless you'd like something stronger."

Min waved his hand dismissively. "Tea is fine."

Sa nodded and hurried back to the bar. Wu watched him go, remembering the times that he had paid rent to the man for the small room upstairs. He hadn't done that in more than two years, not since he had been invited to live in a room in the palace, itself much more spacious than his former accommodations, but not by much. Still, he dined at Sa's establishment, *The Barracks*, at least twice a month, and tried to have any meetings with important government officials within its common room. Both Sa's business and clientele had improved because of those visits, and each time Wu walked through the doors he was greeted with a warm smile, something that still looked out of place on the usually surly proprietor.

"It's true that the army has improved by leaps and bounds over the past two years, but they're still green," Min said, his words drawing Wu's eyes back to him.

"I'm just saying what others are saying," Wu said. "I could really care less if Chu were to attack Yue, and in fact would prefer if they didn't. There is no real need to do it, and I think it's more to assuage Chu's vanity that an invasion is even being planned, not for any practical reasons."

"Be that as it may, the invasion has already been planned and has the full support of Duke Dao. In fact," Min continued as he stroked his small beard, "Duke Dao has a mind to take part in the battle directly, as the lead in one of the chariot wings."

Wu shook his head but held his tongue as Sa returned and put another pot of tea and cup in front of Min before hurrying away.

"Not the best idea, in my opinion," Wu said as he reached across the table to fill Min's cup from the fresh pot.

"Nor mine," Min said as he reached for the tea and blew onto it before taking a sip. "But there's little that can be done to convince him otherwise."

"And his son? He'll surely want to command his own division of the army if his father's doing the same."

"I'm not sure yet what part Su will play in the invasion, but you're probably correct. Su will most likely be given a small command under his father, if not a greater role."

Wu leaned back in his chair, a frown coming to his face. "Why is it that when changes are made within the government, changes that could do so much to lift up the peasantry, they're instead steered directly toward the military?"

"You expected something different?' Min said with a smirk. "Chu has always been a warrior state. If you wanted to do good for the common people perhaps you should have taken your ideas to Qin or Yan."

"Still," Min continued, his smirk disappearing as he leaned forward, "the changes that you advocated to Duke Dao and then brought forth have not been popular with all the segments of society."

Wu sighed. "I'm well aware of that."

"Did you hear what was discussed in the Noble's Council yesterday?"

Wu shook his head. "I rarely pay attention to what they complain about, although I can well imagine what it was." He leaned forward and fixed Min with his eyes. "When I first arrived in Chu there were more than three hundred nobles residing in the city and less than half of that in all the rest of the state. What are there now? A hundred?"

"One hundred and three," Min said.

"There you go," Wu said, sitting back in his chair. "A third of their original number."

"That doesn't make you any safer," Min said quietly. "The things they were saying yesterday-"

"I don't want to hear it," Wu interrupted sharply. "For two years I've been hearing of how unhappy the nobles are with my changes. Each month they level new threats against me from within the safety of their Council. And what they've managed to convince the rest of the state to say about me..." Wu shook his head angrily and gritted his teeth. "I'm sick of hearing about them and their problems. They do nothing for the state but bleed it dry."

"They're sworn to the Duke," Min said. "If ever the Duke needs them they'll come."

"The Duke needed them dearly for years before I came," Wu said angrily, "needed them to curb their wasteful ways and think of that state they were sworn to protect, not how much they could enrich themselves."

Min held up his hands in concession. "Alright, Wu. I agree with you. The nobles were a leech upon the heart of Chu for many years, but that does not mean that they aren't dangerous. And even with two-thirds of them now residing in smaller towns and cities throughout the state, it doesn't mean that they still can't strike against you."

"Why?" Wu said forcefully, drawing a few looks from

the other patrons scattered about the common room. "Why would they come against me, Min? What could they possibly hope to accomplish? Already for two years the changes that I suggested have been carried out, to the betterment of Chu most would agree. And even if they did come against me, killing me perhaps, those changes wouldn't be reversed."

Min shrugged. "I'm just saying what I hear, Wu. Yesterday in the Council Pai Fen and Dao An agreed for the first time in as long as anyone can remember. And do you know what they agreed about, Wu? They agreed how much they hate you, and how something should be done about it."

"So two nobles see eye-to-eye for once; I'm not impressed."

"Not just two nobles, Wu. Pai and Dao are the two most powerful nobles in all of Chu. When they speak things get done, and now that both of them are in agreement you can be sure that something will get done."

"So what are you telling me, Min? That I should go into hiding? Leave the state altogether?"

Min shook his head. "No, I'm just saying that you should be careful is all, perhaps scale back the changes that you're making, or at least some of them."

Wu shook his head. "The changes are already in motion; nothing can stop them now."

Min frowned and leaned back in his chair. Wu Qi had always been a stubborn man, even when he was a lowly soldier rising through the ranks in the Wei Army, as Min had come to learn. Still, it seemed that his reluctance to listen to others had only increased since he had gotten a firm hold on the Duke's ear and his ideas of what would be good for the state were put into action.

And his ideas were good, Min thought as he stared into his tea, thinking on all of the changes that had taken place in such a short time. The nobles had been forced to other areas of the state, something which lessened their stranglehold on the government in Ying and allowed things to actually get done. What's more, government workers, himself, Wu, and the nobles, had all taken significant pay cuts. That had been the most unpopular move, and the first, but when people saw how the saved money was spent, on improving the look of Ying and then the others cities, the grumbling had lessened. When countless peasants began to be lifted up out of a bare subsistence living, the grumbling had ceased altogether. The increased revenue that was generated from so many more people now making a taxable income more than offset what was taken from the government workers, and there was already talk of restoring some of their lost salary, although not by nearly as much as was taken away.

But perhaps the most significant change, the one that played on the consciousness and sense of history of all of Chu's citizens was the lifting up of the army from the sorry state it had been in to one that reminiscent of the glory days of Chu centuries before. At that time Chu had been one of the most powerful states, and people felt pride in its return to that level. The force, which had numbered only a few thousand, now numbered in the tens of thousands. While it was true that nobles still led certain wings and divisions of the army, the majority of the forces were common peasants. Wu Qi had been adamant on that. He had argued vociferously with both Duke Dao and Min about the need to have substantial amounts of foot soldiers. That was the new way of warfare, he had argued, for he had seen it up north. No longer would nobles in chariots be the vanguard of the army; the day of massing forces had arrived, and Chu could either go along with it or be left behind.

Min took another sip of tea. Chu had gone along with it, after much arguing back and forth between the various army commanders, nobles, Duke Dao, and Wu

Qi. In the end Wu got his way and the noble army of Chu became a thing of the past.

"Pai and Dao, you say," Wu said as he stared into his tea. "I'll have to remember those two the next time we move some nobles to the borders."

Min shook his head and chuckled. "You'll never get those two out of Ying."

"No?" Wu peered at Min with narrowed eyes.

"They're too entrenched in the politics of the city, and besides, their families go back for centuries, right here in Ying."

"Anything is possible," Wu said.

Min leaned forward and grabbed hold of Wu's hand.

"Listen Wu, I'm just telling you to be careful is all. These are powerful men that you've angered, and they're used to getting their way."

Wu nodded. "I understand your concern, Min. You've become a good friend to me over the past two years, but you have to understand my position as well. I made a promise to Duke Dao, and more importantly, to myself, that I would change Chu into a state that could be looked upon as an example of what could be done, and example that I hope the other states will follow."

"And you've done that, Wu," Min said, squeezing Wu's hand tighter. "Your place in history is assured. You've proven that a famous general can become a famous administrator. You've thrown your dismissal right back in Marquis Wu's face. What else do you have to prove?"

"Much," Wu said, pulling his hand back and putting it under the table. "Much."

Min shook his head. "I don't think I'll ever understand you, Wu Qi."

"That's not a great burden," Wu said with a smile.

Min gave a half-smile as Wu stood up.

"Now, if you'll excuse me, I'd like to get back to the palace. There's always work to be done."

Min nodded and watched as Wu walked toward the door, the haze of smoke enveloping him.

EIGHT

Pai burst through the door, a servant fast on his heels.

"Sir, you cannot just barge in here like this..."

"They're moving against Yue in two days," Pai said quickly as he reached the desk Dao was sitting behind. He leaned his weight upon it, his hands balled into fists on its smooth surface.

Dai peered up into Pai's eyes then past them to the servant just behind him.

"It's alright, Rai. Pai and I have some important matters to discuss."

The servant bowed his head and stepped backwards to the door, pulling it shut behind him.

"Two days!" Pai cried as he pushed himself off the desk and started pacing the room. "In two days General Min's army will move against Yue. It's our best chance to strike against Wu Qi."

Dai leaned forward in his chair and folded his arms onto the desk. "Slow down. What have you learned?"

Pai paced back and forth across the small room a few more times before he was able to bring his excitement under control enough to stop at the window and peer down onto the street below.

"The army is moving its forces toward Shouchun as

we speak, and they'll be there in force in just two days. From there they'll spill across the border into Yue toward the capital city of Wu. If everything goes right, they should be victorious in a matter of days."

"If everything goes right," Dai repeated skeptically.

Pai turned from the window to look at him. "What could go wrong? The army's been overhauled and re-trained for years now. Our latest reports claim that Chu's forces outnumber those of Yue by nearly three-to-one."

"What could go wrong?" Dai asked, leaning back in his chair to stair thoughtfully at the ceiling. "Well, first of all, we're an invading army that'll be going up against a heavily entrenched force defending its capital. Men have a tendency to fight all the harder when their backs are up against the wall. Secondly, many of these newly trained troops that make up such a large portion of our army have never seen combat and have never raised their swords in anger. How will they perform when the time comes to put their training to the test?"

"They'll perform admirably, I've no fear."

"You're confidence is what is admirable, Pai, although, I fear, a bit misplaced."

Pai moved away from the window and back to the desk, taking one of the chairs that sat in front of it. "So you think they'll lose?"

"I don't so much as think they'll lose, per se; there is a better than average chance that they'll win." Dai leaned forward once again and spoke in a quieter tone. "I think of what would happen if they *did* lose. Where would that put Wu Qi? What would a serious defeat of the army, an army which was recruited and trained according to his orders, do to his high standing and regard within the top tiers of the government?"

"It would most assuredly ruin him," Pai said without hesitation, and Dai nodded.

"But is the ruination of Wu Qi worth that price?" Pai

asked.

"You tell me, Pai. I was under the impression that you hated the man and would do anything to put things back the way they were before he arrived on the scene."

"But ensuring that our army loses? I think that might be too far."

"So now all of a sudden you want Wu Qi and his ideas to prevail, is that it? Tell me, Pai, how much longer will it be before your own family is shipped off to live in some desolate waste of a border town on the pretext that your presence their will make the state safe and strong?"

Pai shifted uneasily in his chair. "It just seems a bit much, is all."

"As were the changes that most of the state was put through over these past years," Dai said.

"So what do you have in mind," Pai said after a few moments of silence.

Dai rose from his chair and walked slowly to the window, peering out onto the busy street below. "It's no longer enough that Wu Qi himself be killed: his ideas have already spread too far into society. The ideas themselves must be killed now, and to do that we have to discredit them. The best way is through our army's defeat."

Dai turned back to face Pai. "Birds will be sent to the Yue Court in Wu, warning them of the invasion. Detailed reports of the army's strength will also be sent, ensuring that the Yue forces can strike back effectively."

"What you propose is treason!" Pai said.

"What I'm proposing is a course that will allow us to return Chu to the way things were before Wu Qi arrived."

"And if your actions are discovered, then what? They'll kill you without pause."

"If *our* actions are discovered," Dai said, "and trust

me, Pai, they won't be."

"But if they are-"

"I thought you wanted Wu Qi gone more than anyone, Pai. Don't tell me that you're suddenly having second thoughts."

"Well, it's just that..."

Dai walked from the window to stand behind Pai. He reached down and began to gently massage Pai's shoulders.

"Yue is a powerful state, one of the most powerful in the Seven States, and one that should, by all rights, be counted among those Seven," Dai said calmly. "It won't come as a great surprise, therefore, when Chu is defeated by them. Wu Qi's ideas were lofty, and perhaps a bit too much too soon. The people will understand." Dai began pressing his fingers into Pai's shoulders more forcefully. "But I can assure you, Pai, that if even a hint of what we have spoken of here today begins to be talked of in the streets, I *will* know who to blame."

Pai tried to sit up in the chair but Dai's powerful hands kept him pressed down.

"There is no backing out now, Pai. You are part of this whether you like it or not."

Dai released his grasp on Pai and the man shot up from the chair. He turned quickly to face Dai, and got a slight smile in return.

"Remember what we've said here today, Pai. You're just as much a part of this as I."

Pai fixed Dai with a challenging stare then hurriedly walked past him to the door of the small office, pulling it open quickly to step outside. Dai watched him go then went back to the window. After a few moments he saw Pai burst out onto the street, walk a few paces, then turn around to look up at the window. Their eyes met and they held gazes. After a moment Pai seemed to let out a deep breath and shrink into himself. He looked back up at Dai in the window and nodded before turning and walking down the street at a slow pace. Dai smiled as he watched him go.

NINE

Wu Qi stared down at his feet for a moment before returning his eyes to Duke Dao.

"You do me a great honor, Sire, but I gave up all military pursuits when I left Wei."

"I would hardly label watching our invasion of the Yue capital a military pursuit," Duke Dao answered.

Wu again lowered his eyes to his feet, trying to think of some way to say no to his ruler without exactly saying the words.

They were in the throne room of the palace, the immensity of it supported by four large marble columns that soared dozens of feet to the ceiling above. A rich white and grey carpet stretched along the marble floor to the only chair in the room, the gold-enameled throne that Duke Dao currently occupied. Standing behind him a few paces was his son and heir, Su Xiong, a young man less than thirty years of age, but who Wu knew from the few times he had spoken with him to be a bright and capable individual, and one that would honorably follow in his father's footsteps.

"Surely you want to see your ideas in action," Su said from behind his father, drawing Wu's eyes up once again. "The army that will take the field in but a few days will be one that you yourself had a hand in making."

"I would hardly say that," Wu began, before Duke Dao raised his hand and cut him off.

"It's true that you did not personally train the men, but it was your training that they followed. Before the army was heavily dependent upon nobles and their chariots, now its true strength lies in the peasant infantry. And they number in the thousands. Surely you'll want to see them take the field."

Wu shook his head. "It does not interest me, Sire."

"Well, then I order you to be present," Duke Dao said, anger edging into his voice.

"As you wish, Sire," Wu said with a slight bow. "May I be dismissed now? If I am to ride on the morrow then I had best be prepared."

"Go," Duke Dao said with a wave of his hand, and Wu turned to walk down the long carpet to the large double doors at the end of the hall. General Min was waiting for him in the hallway.

"So you'll be accompanying us," he said more than asked when Wu emerged from the throne room.

"Looks that way," Wu replied as the two began walking down the long hallway that would lead out of the royal residence and to Wu's own, more humble quarters.

"I don't know why you sound so sullen about it. There was a time when you led men into battle; surely you must miss that."

"No."

Min frowned and hurried to keep up with the fast steps of Wu. "What's the matter, Wu? You knew that your proposals would strengthen the Chu Army, and you knew that would lead to fighting." He chuckled. "That is what armies are for."

Wu stopped and faced Min. "The plans that I proposed and which were adopted did call for a strengthening of the army, but only because that is the only route that common peasants are able to take to lift themselves up from their dreary existence. Believe me, Min, if there were other avenues that the masses could take to better themselves, I would have tried it."

"And what is wrong with the army? It put both you and I where we are today," Min shot back.

"Oh, there's nothing wrong with the army in and of itself," Wu answered. "It's what it's used for that troubles me."

"Armies wage war, Wu. We both know that."

"So tomorrow we move against Yue, and perhaps in another year or two a different state. But what will happen, Min, when there are *no more* smaller states left? Which of the Seven States will be the first to break the peace that was made?"

"That is not for us to worry about, Wu," Min said as they resumed walking and turned the corner leading to Wu's room. "Marquis' and Dukes make those decisions, we just tell the troops what to do when they've been made."

"It doesn't trouble you to know that one day all of the Seven States will find themselves in one large war, a war that will kill tens of thousands, if not more, and leave the country in ruin."

"I don't lose any sleep over it, if that's what you mean," Min said.

Wu shook his head and reached into his robe for the key to his room.

"Wu," Min said, grabbing hold of Wu's arm to stop him. "I *do* think on it sometimes, but truly, those decisions are not up to me. I'm not a ruler of a state, never will be, and never want to. And this war that you speak of so often these days, well, I doubt that it will occur in my lifetime, or the lifetime of my son."

"But it will happen, you *do* know that don't you?"

Min looked down at the floor, but nodded. "It must," he said quietly.

Wu put his own hand on Min's shoulder and walked

him the few feet remaining to his door. "Listen, Min. It's going to be a long day tomorrow. I still have to pack some things, and I know that you have a lot to do. Let's not worry about this now."

Min looked up and nodded. "I'll see you in the morning then. You'll ride with me alongside the Duke's division."

"He's still intent upon leading men into battle?" Wu asked.

Min nodded. "Insists upon it."

"Well, try to steer him away from the heaviest fighting," Wu said as he shook his head.

"Believe me, I will," Min said as he turned to leave. "Now, get some rest, we've a long day ahead of us."

TEN

The sun shone resplendently on the thousands of soldiers marching from the Chu capital, bright rays glinting off of the dagger-axes clutched tightly in the men's hands. Most were outfitted in simple robes stretching from neck to feet, but several wore leather jerkins over their upper bodies. Some men had crossbows hanging from their shoulders, with quivers of bolts on their backs, but most favored the traditional dagger-axes. The weapon consisted of a long wooden shaft the height of a man with an iron dagger affixed perpendicularly at the top. The dagger measured a few inches in come cases, and up to a foot in others. Sometimes the dagger would point only one way while other times it would have a head like an axe. The weapon could be swung, and if the shaft was broken, men could thrust with it.

The column of soldiers stretched for more than a mile as it made its way out of the city. At the head were hundreds of chariots carrying the commanders and other officers, followed by the infantry on foot, more than half of which was still clustered around the city waiting for the long column to stretch out in front of them before they could join its ranks. The road, though wide, could only allow five to six men to march abreast. At that pace it would be nearly midday before all the soldiers were on the move.

Wu Qi and General Min watched it all from a high hill overlooking the city.

"It begins," Min said, his arms folded across his chest and into the long sleeves of his robe. "Your ideas are now a reality."

"It was my idea to lift up a large portion of the peasants, not go after Yue," Wu replied.

"Look down there, Wu. Most of those men marching are peasants, and just a few years ago many of them couldn't even care for their families. You've changed that."

"It'll be awfully difficult to care for their families when they're lying dead in another state."

"Come now, you've got to have more faith in them than that. For two years we've been recruiting and training these men to the standards which you yourself put forth. Sure, many will die, but many more will become even better-off than they are now. When all of the farmlands of Yue are opened up to them they'll want for nothing."

"And what of the Yue peasantry?" Wu asked. "Will they be better off?"

Min turned to face Wu. "Everything will work out."

Wu shrugged and turned away from the sight below. "Let us hope so."

They walked back to the chariot that stood away from the hill's ridge and climbed in. Min took the reins and they were soon racing down to join up with the full road of marching soldiers. They were forced to ride on the rough embankment of the road because of the men, but after a time they reached the head of the column, led by Duke Dao. The Duke was wearing his customary dark grey robes with a long white sash, the tail of which blew behind his racing chariot. All about him were other military officials, men that would command different wings and divisions of the massive army. They'd have command of the parts, but Wu and Min would command the whole

Wu had argued against a place of authority within the army when it was made known that he would be coming to Yue, but Duke Dao would hear none of it.

"You had the ideas, you will lead the men," Dao had said in his throne room the day before.

Wu could tell right away that any argument would be pointless, so he graciously accepted what to any other man would have been a great honor, but to him only seemed a burden.

"Are they all on the road yet?" Dao yelled out when their chariot came up alongside his.

"They're still camped outside the city, waiting for the column to stretch out," Min yelled back in reply. "It'll be midday before they're all moving."

"No matter, it'll take us several days to reach the outskirts of Shouchun. By then all the men will be in place."

Wu hoped that the Duke was correct in his prediction and not just overly confident. Dao had been Duke for less than five years, and had never commanded troops in the field. Wu wished that he could say that Dao still had experience with warfare, but he couldn't. Not since Duke Hui, Dao's great-grandfather, had a Chu leader led men in war, and that had been more than fifty years earlier and in a different time. Duke Hui hadn't had problems with an oversized bureaucracy like Dao had, and at that time the Chu Army had been widely respected by all throughout the Seven States, and feared by many as well. Duke Hui had been a born leader of men in battle, and his long reign, nearly fifty years, had seen the last conquests of Chu against their smaller neighbors. Cai and Chen had been smaller states, but they had also been powerful. No one would have known that, however, by the way that Hui had led his men rolling through their lands. The defenders they found waiting for them there were considered strong and hardy by their neighbors, but only meek to the forces of Chu.

So confident was he in his army that Hui had planned and ordered a dual attack on both neighboring states at the same time. Many men wouldn't have had the confidence to dare such a risky move, but Hui was said to have enough confidence for ten men, and the intelligence to make it true. Within a week both states were no more and Chu had increased in both size and population. Hui himself lived for another twenty years, but it was said that he was filled with depression for much of that time. With no more smaller neighbors to invade and conquer there was little for the Warrior Duke to do but sit in his court and hear the affairs of state, affairs which bored him endlessly and which he had no heart for.

It was during those final decades of his reign that the bureaucracy of Chu began to swell in size and the nobility with it. Hui relegated more and more of the affairs of state to various government officials, many of whom had strong ties to the nobility. The duke only retreated further into himself. During the last few years he barely left his apartments within the Royal Palace at all, and it was said that the smell of his decomposing body was the only way that his servants knew of his death, so reclusive had he become.

None of the military prowess that Hui had exhibited so often and with such zeal on the battlefield was to be found in his oldest son and heir, Duke Jian, Dao's grandfather. By the time his father died and he took the throne, Chu hadn't led a military campaign in twenty years. The states that had already growing in power during Hui's time were now much too powerful for the timid Jian to confront.

It soon became obvious that the greatest threat to Chu was their neighbor to the east, the State of Yue. Having risen to power through the support of Chu more than a century earlier as a counterweight to the growing power of the small State of Wu even further to the east, Yue had eventually grown so strong that it overthrew Wu and supplanted it as the most likely threat to Chu. And that threat had been allowed to grow stronger and stronger under Jian and then his own son and onward to Dao's father, Duke Sheng. Both men had done little to stop the decay of the army or the growth of the bureaucracy and the rising power of the nobility.

Any thought of returning Chu to it previous glory through a military conquest was quickly laughed down, for the army had been allowed to fall into such a disrespectful and sorry state that many believed it couldn't even put down an unruly mob of peasants. The problems with the army had in fact begun during the waning two decades of Hui's rule, for with no enemies to fight, and with Hui having no heart to rule, the nobility and bureaucracy together decided to drastically reduce funding for the military, and the ranks quickly dwindled. Confounding matters was that neither Dukes' Jian nor Sheng had ruled for a substantial length of time. Jian reigned for just over twenty years, but he had done little of consequence to address the problems facing the state during that time. Sheng had tried where his father had failed, but he was already an old man when he took power, and his rein lasted but five short years.

Five years, Wu thought as he looked over at Dao riding in the chariot next to them, the Duke's long queue of black hair blowing behind him. Dao had already ruled for as long as his father had before him, but where he and his own father had failed, Dao had succeeded. *Was* succeeding, Wu immediately corrected himself. While it was true that the power of both the nobility and the bureaucracy had been greatly curtailed, both groups had only been supplanted for a few years and each hungered to regain their former positions. Any misstep, however slight, could create the opening that both needed to claw their way back to the top. And from there they'd once again dwarf the power of the throne.

Wu had tried to ensure such a course would never happen; his whole basis for moving most of the nobles to the Chu borders was because of that. Still, dismissing many of the government officials from the swollen bureaucracy alone just wouldn't be enough. Both groups needed a clear show of force before they'd realize that power no longer resided with them, but with the Duke, where it belonged. A victory against Yue would create that, while a defeat would wipe away all that had been accomplished.

Wu shook his head and tried to dismiss the thoughts. It would not do to dwell on what *might* happen. He was once again riding to war, something that he never thought he would do again, and his thoughts should be there, not back in Ying. Wu nodded to himself and stared straight ahead at the road rushing by, his thoughts once again turning toward war.

ELEVEN

The long column of men came to a stop a few hours before dusk on a bend in the Han River. The river was a tributary of the Jiang River, and they would follow it for most of the next day until they came to the Jiang. From there they'd turn northeast and after another day, possibly two, they would be on the outskirts of the Yue capital of Shouchun.

Min was still pulling the chariot to a stop when Wu jumped off, and almost fell over. His legs were numb from the jarring of the vehicle from the road all day, and it took him a few moments to loosen them up. He stared back down the road as he stretched and was amazed by the sight. Clouds of dust billowed into the air behind them from the hundreds of chariots coming up the road. They grew larger as they joined the clouds formed by the tens of thousands of soldiers walking further behind them, their numbers stretching for miles and miles. It would be fully dark before the last straggled into camp along the river, which by that time would be alight with countless fires and the hum of excited voices.

The lower-ranking officers in the lead chariots immediately staked out a secluded spot on the river atop a small bluff and began erecting the Duke's large tent that would serve as the headquarters and command center of the army. Wu headed to the river to wash the dust from his hands and face. He couldn't remember the last time he'd done that. But he could remember one time.

He'd been riding back north to Wei following the disturbances along the Chu border. He was leading his wing of the army over an eastern mountain pass while Wu Wei, Marquis Wen's son, was leading his wing west. The hostilities between the two villages had easily been suppressed and order restored. There was really no need for the armies of both nations to come at all, except that neither had had much to do at the time.

It had been the day after the dinner with the Chu commanders, and it had been long. It started early with the men breaking camp and didn't end until it was nearly dark and the men were nearing the mountain passes. Wu had ridden ahead to scout the next day's march when he spotted a small stream and steered toward it. He got off his horse and knelt down to the water and washed the dust from his face, just as he was doing now.

Suddenly, he heard the sounds of a rider approaching from the thicket beyond the stream's other side. He got up quickly, not knowing if it was friend or foe approaching. He was just about to draw his sword when he saw Wu Wei burst through the trees and toward the stream's bank.

The two men eyed each other suspiciously for a moment before Wu Wei broke into a smile and jumped from his horse.

"I didn't think I'd find you here," the heir to the throne of Wei said casually. He bent down to the stream's edge and cupped his hands to take a drink. He peered up at the upstart from the State of Qi and narrowed his eyes. "How is she?"

The comment caught Wu off-guard. "She's fine, safe

back in the capital."

"How nice that must be for you, Wu, to come out on top like that."

"Meilin loved me, Wu, not you. Besides, your father never would have approved, didn't in fact. I was amazed to see he let you head up another army. What's it been, more than a year now since you were recalled?"

Wu could remember the incident like it was yesterday, even sitting on the edge of the Han River while marching to war against the State of Yue.

He and Wu Wei had served together when both had been slowly rising through the ranks of the Wei Army. It wasn't unusual for the heir to the throne to serve alongside the common soldiers; in fact, it was encouraged, and there had been a long tradition of it going back over the centuries. While most of the army was composed of men from the State of Wei, not all were. A great deal of the soldiers in all of the armies of the Seven States hailed from different states than those they served.

Wu Qi had been such a soldier. His name was enough to cause him problems back home at the time. The House of Tian was beginning its rise in the State of Qi, and House Jian, which Wu would have fought for, was losing badly at the time. He was lucky to get out with his head.

He had come to the State of Wei and it quickly become apparent that the young soldier from Qi was quite capable. He rose quickly through the ranks, eventually coming to serve alongside Wu Wei in a command position. Both men had had their units sent north against the small state of Cao, and it was there that the troubles between them began.

Both Wu Wei and Wu Qi were men of strong personalities and both sought to outdo the other, pressing their units hard in the fighting, each being rewarded handsomely for their efforts in both victories and recognition. When the state of Cao finally fell and their general met with the defeated duke, both Wu Wei and Wu Qi had been allowed to tag along. It was at that meeting that both men first saw the duke's daughter, and each had been immediately swept under her spell.

She had had hair of auburn and eyes that seemed to penetrate to the depths of their souls. Both men had sought to console her after her father was put to death, and the professional rivalry that had existed between them turned more personal as they sought her favors. Both knew that she was turning the one against the other, but they didn't care. The arguments that had developed between them in the past no longer took place with just words, but with fists. They would have eventually included swords if their general hadn't learned of their quarrels and sent Wu Wei back to Anyi.

"It's been one year, two months, and six days," Wu Wei had said on the bank of the stream that day. "And each of those days I was thinking of you and the humiliation you caused me."

Wu Qi shook his head. "Wu, Meilin and I are married now. In fact, she's expecting our first child, a boy we hope."

"Yes, I know," Wu replied with a smile. "I've known since the day she arrived."

"Then why-"

Wu stopped himself. What game was the heir to Wei playing?

Wu Wei was already walking back to his horse. "And I've had many times to visit her since the day she's arrived. After all, Wu, you've been out of the city a lot lately. I wonder who's been writing your orders?"

Wu Qi's brows furrowed and he looked hatefully at his lord's son. "If you've touched her, Wu..."

He trailed off, leaving the threat unsaid, but surely felt. Wu just laughed as he got back on his horse and turned about.

"I've done a lot more than that since before you were married."

Wu could still hear his laugh as he'd ridden back into the trees. The two didn't encounter one another again on the journey back to Anyi, and Wu was thankful for it. He was still sure he'd have killed the man. Instead he'd rushed back home immediately upon arriving in the city. His wife was there, finally beginning to show her pregnancy. He burst in on her and leveled his accusations right away.

"You've been seeing him," Wu had said, and it still hurt him.

Of course she denied everything, and she might well have been telling the truth; Wu still didn't know to this day. There had never been any time to find out.

"General," a voice called from behind, and Wu Qi turned around.

"General, they're about ready to start the meeting."

"I'll be there," Wu said as he rose up and nodded to the young soldier.

Wu made his way to the tent where the officers were already arguing.

"We must continue on," one officer, a man unfamiliar to Wu, was saying when Wu stepped into the tent.

"That would be folly," another countered. "We must have the battle on the ground of our choosing."

"If we continue east when the Jiang swings south then we'll bypass them altogether," yet another officer said. "Another day of marching should bring us past their troops, whereupon we can swing north toward the capital."

"The capital is now out of our reach," Min said slowly, quieting the other three men and casting his eyes toward Wu near the doorway. "Somehow King Yi of Yue found out about our departure this morning and has sent out the entirety of his army to meet us on the road, if the message we received from our contacts in the city are to be believed."

"Are they?" Wu asked.

Min nodded. "They're reliable."

"How could he have known?" an officer asked.

"He's got spies the same as us," another officer said. "Someone back in the capital told him."

"The nobles, no doubt, at least those that still remain in the city," another chimed in and several men nodded their heads in agreement.

"However it was learned, learned it was, and now we must take the necessary measures to meet this new development," Min said.

"The battle will continue, whether it's at the gates of Shouchun or on the road to it," Duke Dao said, drawing all eyes to him. "Perhaps it was some of the nobles back in Ying that sent word off to King Yi, perhaps it was just advance scouts that he had outside of the city." He shrugged. "Either way it makes no difference now: the battle must take place."

"But where?" one of the officers asked.

Silence reigned in the tent for a few moments as the men's eyes shot between the Duke and Min, and even to Wu. Finally Min snapped his fingers and motioned toward a young soldier near the back of the tent.

"Lay the maps out," Min said as he walked toward the large table set in the middle of the tent.

The soldier quickly jumped to action and in a moment a large map detailing the area between Shouchun and the Yangtze was before them. The soldiers all gathered around the table, watching Min step forward to stroke his neatly-trimmed beard and study the map.

"Here," he said, pointing to a blank spot on the map that looked to be several miles northeast of their current position. "The flat plain the stretches south of Shouchun finally comes to an end here and turns into hills. We could place our archers on the hills overlooking the plain while still affording our chariots ample room to maneuver."

"It's little just over a day's march from Ying," one of the officers pointed out. "If we should be defeated the city will have scarce time to prepare a defense."

"We will *not* be defeated," Duke Dao said as he cast the man a cold look.

"It's nearly a day's march from Shouchun," another man said as he looked at the map. "Even if we are victorious we'll still have to march on the capital, which given a days time, could have put more defenders in place."

Min shook his head. "The reports indicate that the majority of the Yue Army has taken the field. Whatever scant forces remain in the capital will not be sufficient to hold us back."

"What of King Yi?" Wu asked suddenly, drawing all eyes to him. "Is he too riding at the head of his army?"

"We don't know that for sure, but I'd be surprised if he wasn't," Min answered.

"And what will happen if *he* falls in the battle?" Wu pressed.

"Then his forces will scatter, at least that's what we hope," Min said as he looked around at the other men. "King Yi has always been the dominant force that holds the army together. While there's no doubt capable generals will continue the battle, once, and if, the king is slain, I'm sure that the battle will quickly turn in our favor if that eventuality should occur."

"Then we must quickly identify the king and remove him," Wu said.

"That's easier said than done," one of the officers said. "While he may lead one of the initial charges himself, he'll be heavily guarded by his most capable soldiers, men that'll be willing to die for him."

"Our archers then," Duke Dao said.

"Perhaps if we can get a few close enough by chariot, but I don't think there's much possibility of that either," Min said.

"Than what do you suggest?" the Duke asked.

Min stroked his beard once again and leaned over the table. "There is one possibility that might work," he said, pointing toward a small line on the map.

The men gathered as close as they could around the table as Min started to explain, and smiles slowly spread onto their faces.

TWELVE

Lines of heat shimmered in the air as the sun unmercifully beat down. Wu rubbed his forehead with a small cloth that was already nearly soaked through with sweat and peered down on the plain below. General Min stood beside him, although the heat didn't seem to affect him in the least, or if it did, he wasn't showing it. He gazed down at the plain with a determined expression on his face that gave no sign as to his thoughts. Wu's attention was drawn from the plain to the small path they'd climbed. He heard stones skitter and fall and a moment later one of the officers came into view.

"The scouts we sent out have lured the Yue Army this way," he reported when he reached the two men, sweat pouring down his face. "It shouldn't be more than a few hours now."

Wu nodded to the man and the officer rushed back the way he'd come.

"Will we be in position in time?" Wu asked when the man was gone.

"Let's hope so," the general replied, not taking his gaze away from the plain below.

"And if we're not, then what?"

"Then it will be a long day," Min said as he turned to

face him.

Wu nodded and fell in beside as Min began walking back to the path that led down to the plain below. The hill they were on was one of many that overlooked the vast plain stretching out in front of them, the hills rising up on two sides as it finally came to an end after hundreds of miles. The natural boundary had marked the historic border region between the States of Wu and Yue in the times when Chu was itself under pressure from the then smaller state of Wu. Yue had incorporated the former state into its own territory when it had defeated it more than a hundred years before, but the area was still largely uninhabited. as they wound their way down the rocky trail Wu could see why. The plain beneath them allowed only the hardiest of scrub and weeds to find purchase within the dry and rocky land. Although the Jiang and the Han Rivers lay only a few hours to the southwest, they were both far enough away to seem halfway across the world. Still, water was here, and it was for that reason that Min had selected this particular area out of the many miles of hills that made up the area. A small pass wound through the hills where they curved from north to east, and a tiny river, little more than a stream in fact, flowed through before dwindling into nothing, its muddy brown waters sinking into the dry and cracked earth. None in the Army knew the name of the river, so it was simply referred to as 'the river.'

The river was the key to the battle, as Min had outlined back in the command tent the night before. Huddled around the table, the officers and the Duke had listened intently without interruption for more than an hour as Min detailed what would take place the next day. The army would be split in two, with the larger force sent around the northern hills to come up around the Yue Army once it had reached the smaller force awaiting them near the river. It was a risky more. First, their forces, already outnumbered, would be put at a greater disadvantage when they were divided. There was also a strong chance that the larger force wouldn't make the northern pass in time to march south, where it was expected to slam into the rear of the Yue Army. Scouts had been sent ahead that night to make sure that it was possible to get the chariots through, and they had returned well before dawn to say that it was. When they were pressed on how much time it would take to go north, move through the pass, and then swing back south, they became less certain. Some said that it could be done, others that it could not. In the end Min had stuck to the plan, and none had challenged his decision.

The army had been split into two camps the night before and the larger force sent north before dawn. The smaller force, which still numbered in the thousands, continued to march east until they reached the plain a few hours before midday. Even before the sun was fully out the day promised to be hot, but as Wu and Min walked down the trail, dust rising up with each step, it seemed stifling.

"Duke Dao is still intent on leading the initial charge?" Wu asked as they slowly descended to the camps below, their eyes on the trail ahead of them to watch for loose rocks.

"He is," Min said with a sigh. "I've tried to persuade him otherwise, but he'll hear nothing of it."

"He's still a young man, and hungers for the glory that his grandfather and great-grandfather had before him."

"He's apt to get himself killed," Min said.

"The sight of him leading the charge will surely draw King Yi himself out to take the field."

"That's Dao's argument. He says that we can't expect Yi to take the field if he doesn't do so as well."

They walked in silence for a few minutes before Wu asked the question that had been gnawing at him since Min laid out his plan the night before.

"Will the larger force reach the battle in time?"

"Yes," Min said without hesitation.

"You seem quite sure of yourself."

"If I begin to doubt that they will arrive then they will not."

"Oh?"

Min glanced up at Wu and the two men's eyes met. "You know full-well how important confidence is to an army, Wu. If you show even the slightest doubt then the men will sense it and all is lost."

Wu nodded. "Still, it is a long march, the day is hot, and the pass formidable."

"All odds are against us, I know, but Yi's force was already larger than ours before we split the army. He's known about our plans for weeks, perhaps longer."

"Was it the nobles that told him?" Wu asked.

"I don't know who else it could have been," Min said. "We kept the plans for the campaign under wraps until just a few weeks ago when we began to mobilize the troops. While it could have been a spy in the capital that sent off word, I have my suspicions."

Wu nodded. He remembered well the day that Min had warned him of the noble's dislike for him. They hungered for power so much that their allegiance was to themselves first, and to Chu second. If the army was defeated they would view that as a victory for themselves, a rebuke of all of the changes that Wu had instituted over the past two years. They didn't seem to consider that a loss in the field against Yue could mean disaster for Chu, possibly the elimination of the State altogether. Wu had no doubt that King Yi would march straight to Ying if they lost the battle today. If Duke Dao was lost things would only be worse.

The trail came to an end at the bottom of the hill and before them stretched hundreds of tents set up by the soldiers. Cheers rose and the talk became excited as they made their way toward the center of the camp. All about them men were honing the edges of their weapons and checking over their armor; anything to keep the anxiety of waiting at bay. Each of the soldiers knew that they would be fighting in only a few hours, and they meant to be ready.

The command tent was given ample space within the throng of other tents and several guards stood sentry outside. Wu and Min were each given a nod as they approached and then went inside. A large table dominated the center of the tent, the map of the area taking up much of its surface. Duke Dao was bent over it, poring over the detailed terrain, officers all about him.

"Any word from the scouts?" Min asked as he walked up to the table.

"A few reported back just a few minutes ago," one officer said. "Yi's men continue their march south to meet us; there's been no change there."

"And the pass?" Min knew that if any advance scouts of the Yue Army smelled out the Chu soldiers on the other side of the hills then their plan would be finished.

"It appears that the main body of their army is moving right past it," the officer said.

"A small detachment, numbering little more than a hundred men, has been left to guard it," another officer said.

Min nodded and gave a sigh of relief. "And what of our own forces? Have they reached the pass yet?"

The officer looked down at the floor of the tent before meeting Min's eyes. "The only reports we have from them are a few hours old. At that time they expected to reach it within a few hours and begin moving through before midday."

Min nodded at the man's words. "How are the emplacements on the plain going?"

Another officer stepped forward. "We've got the archers already moved into place in the low hills overlooking the plain. They're a mile north of us and will fire down on the approaching army."

Min nodded again. He hoped that the fire from the hills would draw a large portion of Yi's men away from the plain, enough that when Chu's chariot and infantry charge swept forth Yue's forces would be slightly divided.

"And the infantry? They've not been placed yet."

"They'll move up within the hour," another officer stepped forward to report.

"And then the chariots will advance," Duke Dao said as he walked over and put a reassuring arm around Min's neck. "Don't worry, Min, we're following your plan just as you wanted. Still, I have to admit, I'm a bit uneasy. Yi's men will outnumber us by nearly three-to-one at first. Even if we do manage to hold them, it will be some time before our second wing reaches the battle from the pass."

"That's all we can do at first, hold them," Min said. He turned to the officer that had spoken up about the infantry. "The men know how their formations are to break and pull back after the initial engagement?"

The man nodded. "They've been drilled repeatedly about their role in falling back beyond the river."

"The chariots can still go around the river," Duke Dao said to Min.

"I hope they try. Any attempt to move up along the river will first open them up to our archers. Then if they manage to come up and around where the river ends so as to fall back on our forces they'll have to do so in a nearly single-file formation. There's just not enough room between the rise in the hills and the river for much more than two chariots to move down at a time."

"If we incapacitate just a few of their chariots when they make that move then the path will be blocked to them," Min added.

Duke Dao nodded. "It's a good plan, but one that I'm not wholly convinced Yi will adhere to. He'll no doubt sense the trap."

"Their chariots outnumber ours by too high a margin for us to allow them the advantage of mobility," Min replied.

"Well, it shouldn't be much longer now," Dao said as he folded his arms into his robes and looked at each of the men in the tent.

"I wish you would reconsider leading the charge," Min said.

Dao shook his head. "My place is with the men, not sitting in the rear watching the battle from afar."

"The risk is too great, at least until our main force arrives from the pass," Min pleaded.

Dao clapped him on the back. "Min, the decision is mine. I *will* lead a charge."

Min nodded sullenly. He had a bad feeling about his Duke's eagerness to partake in the battle, but at the same time a good-deal of admiration. Many of the rulers of the Seven States shied away from leading troops into battle; that couldn't be said of Duke Dao of Chu.

"And when the battle is finished?" Wu asked, speaking for the first time.

"That is difficult to say," Min answered. "If we still have the numbers I expect to continue the march on Shouchun."

"There is a good chance that King Yi will escape the battle unscathed. He'll return to the capital and rally the people to him." Wu stared hard into Min's eyes. "The fighting there will be fierce."

"Old men and boys are all that remain back in the capital," Dao said with a laugh that was quickly echoed by the other officers in the tent. "If Yi does make it back to Shouchun, I think the last thing we need to worry about is a determined resistance."

"Not with the majority of his men marching to meet us in the field," one of the officers said.

"Still, there is a chance-"

"The attack will be pressed," Min said sharply, cutting Wu off. "Shouchun will be taken."

"That's the attitude I like," Dao said with a laugh and another clap on Min's back.

Wu nodded. They were confident, that much was for sure. Deep down, however, he felt ill-at-ease. If pressed on how he felt, he wouldn't have been able to say, only that there was a feeling something wasn't right. A foreboding was what it was, and he knew it well from when he led Wei Army soldiers into battle. He came to recognize the feeling, and knew that it presaged catastrophe. He'd had the feeling many times before, and it hadn't always come before a loss, but also when a victory wasn't quite complete. Either a large portion of the enemy's army had gotten away, a leading general fled, or his own forces were so decimated that the victory seemed more defeat than anything. Each time before those battles he had had the same feeling in the pit of his stomach that he was having now. Watching the officer's laugh and joke with their Duke and general, however, gave Wu the impression that it would do little good bringing it up. Even with Min, he realized, someone that he had grown comfortable sharing his feelings with over the years, the trepidation would be unwelcome. Best to swallow the feeling and hope that it went away. And hope even more that what it foretold was nothing more than heavy losses as would be expected with such a battle.

A soldier suddenly rushed into the tent, his chest heaving for breath. "The advance wing of Yi's men have been spotted, they'll be on us in little more than an hour."

The joking and laughter died at the words and all eyes went to Dao and then Min. Min looked from the man to Dao to each of the officers in what seemed a single moment.

"Get into position," he said quietly.

No words were said as each of the officer rushed from the tent and toward whichever division of the army they were to command. Duke Dao was about to follow them out when Min stayed him with a touch on the arm.

"We have an hour, Sire," Min said. "Let us go up the hills a ways and see these forces with our own eyes."

Dao nodded and fell in behind Min as he left the tent, Wu close on his heels. They were the only men moving away from the plain, it seemed, as they made their way south through the camp toward the hills that afforded a clear view for miles down the plain. All about them soldiers rushed to pick up their weapons and armor before hastily heading to whichever area had been appointed as their rallying point. Horses snorted and dug their hooves into the ground at all of the frantic activity about them before men pulled them along. Most would be used to pull the hundreds of chariots that were already waiting on the northern outskirts of camp, while several dozen would hold single riders appointed with circling around the battle and reporting back to the officers and general on the latest developments.

Few men seemed to notice that their Duke was moving about among them, heading in the opposite direction of where the battle would take place, and after a few minutes of dodging men and animals alike the three reached the edge of the southern hills and the trail that ascended up their rocky slopes.

They only had to walk a few hundred yards up the trail before they saw the enemy forces. The chariots came first, large clouds of dust swirling upward into the air in their wake, the rows upon rows of infantry marching several miles further behind. Even from this distance the heat seemed to shimmer and reflect off of the thousands of dagger-axes the infantry held.

"They'll be here within the hour," Dao said in alarm

when he saw how close the chariots were.

"The chariots, yes," Min replied, "but I doubt they'll do much more than wait a good distance away from us until the infantry catches up. I expect they're trying to rattle our nerves with this first appearance."

"I can't even see the end to that column of infantry," Dao said, pointing at the dark brown blocks marching slowly toward them.

"They're formed into three columns," Wu said, bending over to point so that Dao could follow his finger. "Two blocks of men to each column, with each block comprising...oh, about three thousand men, I'd say."

"Sounds about right," Min said.

Dao looked from Wu to Min and back to where Wu was pointing. "Three thousand in each of those moving squares? There must be a dozen of those squares of men."

"Eighteen," Wu corrected. "Three squares in each line, two lines to each column. Three columns make eighteen blocks of infantry, or about fifty-four thousand men."

"Fifty-four thousand," Dao said quietly. "We've got what? Scarcely half that?"

"Just under twenty thousand," Min answered, "each set into divisions of five thousand men."

"They'll march right over us!" Dao nearly shouted.

"Not if we fall back onto the river, and don't forget about the archers in the hills. One good archer can take out a dozen infantrymen in little more than a minute."

"And remember, we're simply going to hold Yi's men until the other wing of the army swings south from the pass and marches on their rear," Wu pointed out.

"I'm beginning to have doubts as to whether we'll be able to hold them that long," Dao said.

"Don't," Min said brusquely. "The men need your confidence and will smell your doubt and fear a mile away. If you mean to lead the men in a charge you have to do so with the dead-certainty that you *will* be victorious."

Dao nodded and swallowed the knot in his throat. "We'd better get down there, then. It looks like we'll be fighting in an hour's time."

Duke Dao began descending the trail before they could say anything, his head held high. Min glanced at Wu, shrugged, and started down after him. Wu paused for another moment to look at the forces slowly making their way south and the forces quickly assembling to meet them, then glanced again at Duke Dao. Min was right about the men being able to sense their commander's doubts and fears, but he wasn't quite sure Duke Dao had managed to quell his yet.

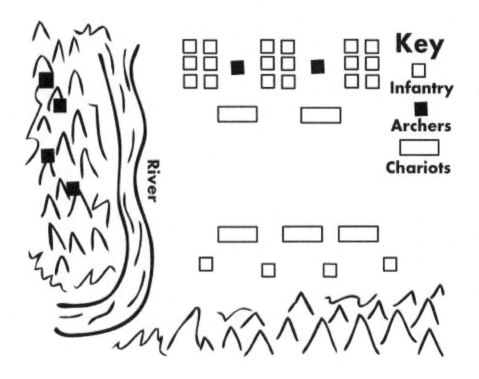

The Battle on the Plains

THIRTEEN

The Chu Army had four divisions of infantry that numbered nearly five thousand men each. They were arrayed east of the river in a line a few hundred yards ahead of the camp. In front of them were the three chariot divisions which numbered two hundred and fifty each. In the northern hills to their west were the four divisions of archers, five hundred men in each. It was a sizable force, but Wu was not sure it would be enough.

He held the reins of a chariot in his hands, trying his best to keep the two skittish horses under control. A low-ranking officer named Chou stood on the platform next to him, a bow held at his side. His primary duty was to fire at any enemy archers riding in the opposing chariots, though Wu also tasked him with keeping his eyes on Duke Dao as much as possible. The Duke was in the next division over from them, on their right and in the middle of the three divisions, and although Wu knew that several chariots would be given over wholly to protecting the Duke, he figured one more couldn't hurt.

Min drove a chariot in the third division on the rightmost flank, from where he would be in command of the army. While it's true he'd riding about in the battle, his primary task was to ascertain how the enemy was faring. A dozen chariots were to stay out of the fighting entirely and only ride about, viewing the shifting lines and gauging the positions of both forces. Wu had commanded armies before in the State of Wei, and he knew from experience that Min would be bombarded by reports continuously.

Ahead of them the State of Yue's Army was still assembling, though they had brought the majority of their forces into place. Five divisions of chariots, which Wu thought to number nearly three thousand, stood in front of the three massive columns of infantry, which numbered more than fifty thousand men. Between the columns of infantry were two divisions of archers, which looked to number around two thousand, the only numbers which matched their own. Chariots were still moving into place, and nearly the entirety of the vast columns of infantry were concealed in clouds of dust, something Wu thought was for the best; it wouldn't do to have their own infantry get too nervous at the sight of such overwhelming odds facing them.

The odds would even out once their main force reached them from the northern pass. The scouts had reported that the force had begun moving through the pass more than an hour ago, but it was still a march of many miles down the plain before they would reach the battle. The majority of that force was infantry. The four divisions of men would have to rush down to get to the battle in time, something that wouldn't be easy in the stifling heat. The chariots that led them would also have to go slow. It wouldn't do to have half of the large force appear, giving away the surprise and possibly being routed, before the infantry even arrived.

Still, Wu knew the odds were heavily stacked against them. Even when, or if, the northern division of the army reached them, they'd still be heavily outnumbered. The State of Wu's army had just under

60,000 men. The State of Chu's army had just over 41,000 men, and half of them were currently marching through a mountain pass. Right now Chu was fielding a force of just over 21,000 men against an army that outnumbered it nearly 3-to-1.

General Min was in charge of the battle, something that he had talked repeatedly about with Duke Dao. The Duke had agreed, but Wu knew full-well that the course of the battle could change that. The plan was to wait for the Yue Army to march upon them, coming at them first with volleys of arrows and a chariot charge. The Chu Army would hold for as long as possible, their archers firing down on the advancing troops from the hills above, before the chariots would make a combined thrust at the left flank of the Yue Army, driving into the ranks of infantry. While that happened the right flank of the Chu infantry would pull back across the river, each division pulling back in turn. The most important factor would be deciding when to have the chariots charge the left flank. Min was to give that order, and Wu hoped that Duke Dao waited for it.

A great cheer arose from the army ahead of them, the soldiers no doubt pepped-up by their commanders. Nearly all of the chariots were now in place nearly a mile from them, Wu could see; it wouldn't be much longer. He felt rather calm, something that always struck him as a bit odd. Most men he knew, even seasoned veterans of battle, became quite fearful before the initial charge. Not Wu. He had somehow developed the capacity for calm after years of war. That wasn't the case with the officer next to him. Wu could see the man's hand turning white from how forcefully he gripped the top of the chariot, while the hand held at his side was visibly trembling. Wu put his hand on the man's shoulder.

"Don't let them make you nervous with their shouting, Chou," Wu said. "They're yelling to try and make their own fear go away."

"I'll try not to, General," Chou said shakily and with a smile that quickly turned back to a frown.

Wu patted him on the back again then looped his hands through the reins. The Chu Army officers were already moving about their own men, rallying them with impromptu speeches on what awaited their victory. Similar shouts were coming from the ranks of infantry behind them, but they weren't nearly as loud or adamant as those heard from across the sun-baked plain.

Just let them hold long enough for the main force to arrive, Wu thought as he stared through the shimmering heat waves at the army waiting to destroy them.

And then it came, the final loud cheer and then the deafening rumble as three thousand chariots began their charge. It was as if the men a mile away had stolen the men's voices, so quiet did it become in the first ranks behind Wu. He could feel the familiar pounding in his chest, the echoing rumble of thousands of horses on the hard-packed earth.

He paid it no heed. He'd grown accustomed to that sensation, having led the charge more often than not, although he had been on the receiving end his fare share of the time. The men behind him, however, had never experienced it before. Wu glanced back and was happy to see that the ranks remained firm, that no men had dropped their weapons and fled in fear. It was a disciplined force that had been put together over the past two years, but Wu still saw more than a few stained breeches from men unable to hold their bladders along with their courage.

He turned his head back to the plain in front of them and saw that the chariots were in a full-out charge. *King Yi must be confident indeed,* Wu thought, for he was not even bothering with his archers. Behind the swirling clouds of dust he could just make out the infantry beginning their fast march onto the field.

His eyes went to the north hills on their left. Two thousand archers were waiting in the rocky outcroppings, and they had a clear line of fire down onto the plain below. For some reason the Yue army hadn't concerned themselves with the men, perhaps thinking them ineffective against such a larger force. *We'll see about that*, Wu thought with a smile. The men on the hills had been trained well; Wu had watched them during practice both in Ying and in their camps at night so knew that each man could draw and fire more than five shots a minute with deadly accuracy. Still, it was several hundred yards from the hills to the plain below, and they were firing at moving targets.

The Yue chariots were just about in line with that first division of five hundred archers when the air became filled with arrows. They had been aimed well ahead and flew out into the sky in a wide arc soaring up and out before turning down into a torrent of death. The first volley was right-on, and Wu watched as more than a dozen chariots flipped over, their horses, drivers, or both impaled by the arrows. A dozen wooden shafts sprouted from chariot carriages with occupants lucky not to have been hit, and the vehicles sped on, right into line with the next division of archers atop the hill. Again the rain of arrows came down, and again several dozen chariots met a crashing end. Still, even with a hundred or more chariots taken out in such a fashion, nearly three thousand remained, and those quickly corrected their course, steering to their left so as to avoid the deadly barrage from above.

All along the Chu line horses were kicking and stomping their hooves into the ground, and a few even reared up, knocking over their chariots, but the majority held the line. Wu glanced down the lead line of chariots, and even though he couldn't make out Min on the far right flank, he knew that the general was gritting his teeth as he watched the enemy chariots come closer and closer. Already they were past the second division of archers on the hill and just a few hundred yards from the mouth of the river.

And then the call came and before he even realized it, Wu was cracking the reins down on the two horses in front of him and his chariot was rushing forth to battle.

From the hills the third division of archers let loose, and Wu saw several more chariots crash out of the advancing line, their riders thrown out of the carriages to be trampled to death by the vehicles next to them. Even with a few hundred chariots taken out by archers the Yue line continued to advance rapidly.

Two hundred yards, then one hundred; on they came. Wu could hear the shouts of the men on both lines of the battle and then he was crashing through the line of the enemy and they through his. Horses skittered and cried all around and within moments the air was filled with the sounds of swords and dagger-axes ringing against one another. Wu was surrounded by enemy chariots but didn't even think. With one hand tightly woven around the reins he grabbed his sword and began swinging while beside him Chou dropped his bow to his feet and took up his own sword.

Their only hope was to fight through the line of chariots before the Yue infantry arrived behind them, cutting off all escape. Wu cracked the reins and tried his best to drive the chariot forward as he swung his sword at the men in chariots beside him. Blood sprayed as he severed on man's sword arm. He took another through the chest with a savage thrust.

Chou cried out beside him and Wu glanced over in time to see him block two overhead swings from a soldier on the chariot over. Chou was fast, though, and drove his own sword into the man's stomach as the man tried to raise his sword for another swing. Wu turned away as the red and white guts of the man began to flow from the savage wound, and thankfully just in time to block a swing aimed at his head. Steel rang against steel as he parried and blocked his newest assailant's attacks with both his sword and chariot, but before either was able to land the killing blow their chariots were past one another. The press of chariots around them was loosening and Wu found that he suddenly had more mobility. He cracked the reins hard and steered toward an opening ahead. A few final swings from his and Chou's swords and they managed to cut their way out of the battle.

Wu tugged on the reins and paused for a moment after they made it past the fighting. Dust swirled all about but Wu could see that the Yue infantry was still several hundred yards away, although marching fast. Arrows rained down on them from above, causing hundreds of men fell with each volley, but they continued on. Even if the archers managed to kill several thousand men before the whole force reached the main battle there would still be tens of thousands ready, their blood up at the loss of their companions.

Behind them the battle raged, and Wu could hear that their own infantry had already joined the fight in the rear. It was still largely chaos, neither side having recovered from the initial charge enough to sort out their lines and divisions. Wu was not tasked with leading a division, which would have been nearly impossible anyway given the confusion of battle lines at the moment, so he whirled the chariot around the seething mass of men and horses toward their right flank. It was there that he expected to find Min and hopefully Duke Dao as well.

"Fire at the officers!" Wu yelled out above the din of battle as he raced eastward.

"Which ones are the officers?" Chou yelled back as

he dropped his sword and reached for his bow.

"The ones with swords!" Wu yelled.

Chou may not have known much about the make-up of the opposing military ranks, but he more than made up for it by his skill with the bow. Before they had gone another fifty yards he had already struck three enemy swordsmen who were wildly swinging away from their chariots. Each man fell with an arrow through the throat.

It quickly became apparent that all semblance of command was lost in the swirling chaos of the battle and that Wu would have a hard time finding Duke Dao or Min's location. He kept the chariot moving, however, and was soon on the edge of the battle and circling down into his own ranks.

"There!" Chou called out, pointing with his arm toward a cluster of chariots off to the side.

Wu looked and saw that it was Min, doing his best to direct the action of his men. Wu cracked the reins and within a minute was alongside the group.

"Firm up the ranks!" Min was shouting at the chariots around him. "Get the infantry moving back across the river!"

Wu was surprised that Min was giving the order to fall back so quickly in the battle, but one glance back at the swirling mass of chariots and infantry told him that they were dangerously outnumbered and at risk of being overrun. The enemy infantry would be on top of them in minutes, and if they didn't break now there'd be a good chance that they would be surrounded and swallowed up.

"Where's Dao?" Wu yelled to Min when he was alongside his chariot.

"We've lost sight of him," Min yelled back between orders.

Wu frowned and stared back into the maelstrom of battle. For every one of their chariots he saw a dozen of the enemy's.

"We've got to get in there and get him out!" Wu yelled.

"Go, and give the order to fall back to all that you can," Min yelled back, his attention already back to the men around him.

Wu cracked the reins and headed back into the swirling mass of men and animals, shouting for the men to fall back as he plunged into the chaos. Chou dropped his bow and again picked up his sword, swinging and stabbing as they steered around upturned chariots and drove over fallen men, many writhing in pain from their wounds. All the while Wu called out the orders for the men to pull back and regroup across the river. His words were having an effect, at least; already large groups of infantry were moving back toward the river, the chariots doing their best to take the brunt of the fighting so as to allow them an escape.

As Wu drove deeper into the ranks of infantry and enemy chariots he began to lose hope that he'd spot Duke Dao, but then suddenly he saw him, still atop his chariot, a ring of infantry and chariots around him. He seemed to be directing the attack, and the battle was going favorably around him, although Wu didn't know how long that'd be the case, especially when the Yue infantry arrived.

"Pull back!" Dao was yelling. "To the river!"

Wu managed to get close enough and Dao spotted him.

"Has Min given the order?" he yelled out as Wu steered through the protective ring to com up alongside.

"He has," Wu yelled back. "The infantry are already pulling back while the chariots hold."

Dao nodded and looked around him. "The enemy infantry, how long?"

"They'll be on top of us in minutes," Wu replied. "We've got to get you out of here."

Wu saw the Duke grit his teeth and frown, not happy with the thought of leaving his men.

"If we don't get you out of here when the infantry arrives then you'll be swallowed up!" Wu yelled. "The men *need* you to stay alive and command them."

That did it. Dao nodded and tightened his hands about the reins of his chariot. "Lead me to Min, then."

Wu nodded and put his chariot into motion, glancing back to see that Dao was following behind. The ring of men and chariots advanced with him, although when the enemy chariots saw that the Duke of Chu was moving past them they quickly descended. The infantry were the first to be cut down, but most of the chariots managed to make it through. Within moments they were out of the heaviest of the fighting and advancing upon Min's position.

"Are the infantry pulling back?" Min shouted when Wu was close enough to hear.

"They are, and the chariots are coming this way, as many as remain," Wu replied loudly over the sounds of battle.

"The Yue infantry are already too close for us to make it to the mouth of the river," Min said. "We'll have to circle around their whole army."

"Can we do that?" Dao asked. "They still have their archers in reserve."

"It's our only choice," Min said. "We have to protect the area between the river and the hills. If we don't the enemy chariots will have a straight path down onto our infantry."

"Then lead us around," Dao said.

Min nodded and steered his chariot north. With a last glance back behind him he cracked his horse's reins and put the chariot into motion, the rest quickly doing the same. Wu glanced about. No more than two hundred chariots comprised their division, the rest still fighting it out in the middle of the field, trying to buy the infantry as much time as possible to get

across the river. Once there the men would be safe
from the enemy chariots, which would have to circle
around the mouth of the river and come down the
narrow corridor between the water and the hills. The
bulk of the enemy infantry would most likely try and
fight their way across the river, which was narrow and
shallow enough to stop low-lying chariots, but not men
on foot. It would be a tough fight, and one that they
hadn't anticipated getting into so quickly. The Yue
forces were better-organized and more powerful then
they'd thought. Wu gave a silent prayer to Shangdi
that their main force was running south to join them.

As they broke north many of the enemy chariots
disengaged as best they could from the fighting to
pursue. Chariots were fierce weapons when allowed
the mobility that was their main feature, but when
surrounded by infantry they quickly became bogged
down and were easy to defeat. The Yue forces knew
this well, and at the sight of the Chu chariots speeding
north toward their own fast-approaching infantry
lines, they too sped north. The respite from the
fighting allowed the Chu infantry to pull back en
masse and gave an opportunity to those Chu chariots
still in the midst of battle to disengage themselves and
head toward the mouth of the river on their own. *At
least he's saving his army*, Wu thought as he glanced
over at Duke Dao.

Within moments of breaking north they were
speeding past the Yue infantry divisions.

"Take up your bow and take out as many of them as
you can," Wu yelled to Chou over the rumble of wheels
all about them.

Chou once again put down his sword and picked up
his bow. He sidled around Wu and nocked an arrow,
taking careful aim before firing. Even with the shaking
of the chariot there was little chance that he would
miss; the Yue infantry was arrayed in the thousands
all alongside of them and made easy targets. Wu saw

other arrows flying out from the chariots around him, as well as those still raining down from the hills above. A large section of the Yue left flank disengaged from their march to swing into the path of the advancing chariots. While many men would be killed if more than two hundred chariots slammed into them, there numbers were enough to ensure that they could stop the whole force in a manner of minutes. Ahead of them Min saw the move and steered them well clear, their horse-drawn chariots faster than even the most capable runners in the infantry. Still, there were thousands of men in the lines, and it took them some time to pass to the rear of the column.

There they found a new set of problems: directly behind the infantry were the two large divisions of archers, already in place and readying their bows to fire upon the hills where the Chu archers were embedded. And coming down directly beside them, and right at the advancing column of Chu chariots, were several hundred enemy chariots. Wu's mouth came open at the sight; either King Yi had held a large portion of his chariots in reserve or they had already broken off from the fighting in the middle of the field and somehow gotten up and around their own infantry. It was a large dilemma, and Wu knew that they were trapped. Behind them came hundreds of chariots, to their left were thousands of infantry men, and ahead of them were archers and even more chariots. The only route open to them lay to their right, a direction which would take them further from the fighting still taking place in the middle of the field, and the river mouth where their presence was so urgently needed.

Ahead of them Min reined up his horses and slowed his chariot. Duke Dao was in the chariot next to him, and after a moment Wu was able to steer up alongside as well.

"We'll make a break right behind the infantry," Min

yelled out to them. "Scatter as many of the archers as you can to buy our men in the hills more time."

"It'll be close," Wu yelled back. "If enough of those archers stand their ground it'll impede our movement and allow some of the infantry and chariots to close the gap in front of us. We'll be trapped."

"It's a risk we'll have to take, and quickly," Min yelled back as he gripped his reins tightly. "Besides," he added with a smile, "when have you ever known archers to hold their ground?"

Min cracked the reins and sent his chariot into the thin gap between the south-marching infantry and fast approaching chariots from the north. Wu smiled despite himself as he watched him go; the man was actually enjoying this, he realized. Wu yelled out and cracked the reins, sending the chariot into motion behind Min and Dao, a newfound burst of confidence upon him.

FOURTEEN

Wu quickly realized that confidence was needed, and hoped that the drivers of the chariots behind him got a piece of it as well. Ahead of them stood more than two thousand archers, on either side of which were infantry and chariots. Riding in front, Min cracked his reins repeatedly, trying to get every last ounce of speed from the two horses pulling him, while beside him Duke Dao did the same. Already the rear ranks of the Yue infantry saw what they were attempting and were turning about to impede their progress. It was an uncoordinated move, however, one lacking in leadership and direction, and the men would most likely be unable to come into any type of blocking stance until they reached the last of the three long columns. The chariots were another matter entirely. Driven by disciplined officers who could make decisions on their own, they quickly turned their cars about to block the path before the Chu chariots reached their archers. It would be close, Wu quickly saw, but he didn't think they would pull into position in time to block their first few ranks, and he suspected that only a few dozen of their two hundred chariots would by stymied by the attempt.

A new concern quickly replaced that posed by the

chariots. Instead of running like most men would, the archers were determinedly standing their ground, grabbing arrows from their quivers and nocking them to their bows. Already men were aiming at them, and a few arrows flew over their heads as they got closer. Wu saw Min yell something to Dao that he could not make out, and which the Duke only shook his head at. A moment later Min began steering his chariot into a more direct line with the archers, the movement forcing Dao to do the same with his own chariot. Wu made the same maneuver, and glancing over his shoulder he saw that the others in line behind him were making it as well. When he returned his eyes to the archers ahead of them he saw the first few men begin to break ranks and run. They were quickly followed by more as their column of chariots got closer, and by the time they were within a hundred yards all of them had taken to their heels.

Wu would have smiled but for the chariots quickly filling the gap left by the archers. The Yue chariots were plowing right through the retreating ranks of archers, heedless of the fleeing men's safety in their rush to break the enemy's charge. Min and Dao and then Wu quickly flew by the advancing cars, but Wu could tell that the main thrust of that force would bear down on his companions just a few chariots behind.

Min tried to buy them speed and time by cracking his reins repeatedly, especially after they heard the first wing of Yue chariots slam into them further back down their long line. Wu had thought that they would lose only a few dozen to that chariot charge; now he realized that it was only a few dozen that would survive. Shouts and cries erupted in their rear as their men were surrounded. There was nothing they could do, however; to turn back and fight would mean certain death for themselves and defeat for the entire army. They had to press on, and that's exactly what Min did.

They plowed through the fleeing archers and ran over any foolish enough to hold their ground. Arrows still flew at them, but most were high, while the few well-aimed embedded themselves in the cars more often than not. The threat of the chariots and archers behind them, they still found they had one obstacle to contend with, and that was the large cluster of infantry now blocking their path. They were already passing the second column of infantry, but the third had found enough time to pull some men back in an attempt to stop the chariot charge. It was too late however, for even with the archers regrouping in their rear and ready to fire down on them as they rushed to the river, their whole right flank was clear. Min simply steered them up and around the men and they were quickly heading back south, the mouth of the river, and their own ranks of infantry, before them. Wu had never seen a more welcome sight.

The ranks cheered them when they wheeled into their midst, the few that were not busy fighting it out over the river. Min pulled up on his reins and brought his chariot to a halt well into their ranks and quickly hopped out of the car. He stood staring back at the few chariots coming in behind him, and Wu saw him shake his head sadly as he brought his own horses and car to a halt and handed the reins to Chou.

"I didn't think we had lost so many," Min was saying to Dao when Wu walked up. "Where those chariots came from I don't know."

"Yi had them in reserve," Wu quickly said. "I thought more would get through as well."

The three men stood and watched as the last of the chariots came in behind them. Wu did a quick count and was appalled. Of the more than two hundred that had broken free of the fighting in the field to rush north and around the infantry, less than fifty remained.

"We won't be blocking the mouth of the river with

this force," Min said sadly. He waved over one of the nearby officers. "Get a division of infantry up to block the mouth of the river," Min said to the man when he reached them.

The officer nodded and ran off toward the sound of fighting coming from the river to their right. Min watched him go before turning to look around.

"There's got to be some type of command here," he said.

Wu glanced about but could see no such thing. They were on the very edge of the first division of infantry, the one furthest away from the fighting that was raging somewhere south of them.

"Further down the river, most likely," Dao said. "A chariot will take us the length of the line more quickly."

Min nodded and wiped the dust and sweat from his face, and Wu saw for the first time how dazed and tired the man truly was. The battle had obviously taken its toll on him, especially the loss of the chariots. They had started the battle with seven hundred and fifty, and, unless some had escaped from the fighting to come across the river on their own, they were now down to a few dozen. Wu had no idea what shape their infantry was in, but if the ferocity of the fighting from the field was any indication, they had also taken a hard hit. The only force that appeared unscathed were their archers, still high atop the hills on their left, but who would no doubt be forced to scatter once the Yue archers got reorganized and fired upon them.

The infantry was the real question, however; without them they had nothing. They'd started the battle with nearly twenty thousand. If all of divisions had managed to get across the river they would be able to hold for some time; long enough, Wu hoped, for their main force to finish its long march from the northern pass. They would soon find out, Wu knew as they walked to Dao's chariot, the Duke taking the reins and putting them into motion.

The two divisions of Chu infantry closest to the river when the battle had started had managed to make it across when the order had been given. As the three men went by in their chariot the soldiers cheered them, happy to see their Duke and leading general still in the fight. Already they were moving further up toward the river's mouth to block the chariots they knew would come. The further they rode down the river, however, the worse things became. Half of the third division of infantry had made it across the river, but the other half was in the process of making its way across or still on the plain fighting. The fourth division was wholly across the river, unable to break away from the chariots that assaulted them. By this time the main force of the Yue infantry had reached the river and was slamming hard into the Chu infantry. Officers tried to rally the men and get them across the river, where they would at least by away from the chariots, but in the chaos of the fighting it just wasn't happening. Bodies floated in the shallow river which was already turning red with blood.

"We've got to get those men across!" Dao shouted out when they came upon the thick of the fighting.

"We can't risk sending the other two divisions into the river to aid them," Min yelled back. "The rest of the Yue infantry will be down upon them in moments anyway."

"So we just leave them to die out there?" Dao shouted.

"No, we leave them to fight," Min shouted back.

They came to the end of the line where the fighting had yet to take hold and Dao swung the chariot back around, bringing it to a stop.

"There's no point in all three of us riding in one chariot," he said. "Min, I want you to get into another car and rally these men still across the river. Wu and I will go aid in the stand against the chariots."

Min only nodded and jumped out onto the ground. He waved down one of the chariots that had been following them and hopped in while it was still moving. Dao glanced over at Wu and cracked the reins, sending them back toward their left flank near the river's mouth.

They were still passing by the third division, itself still trapped in and on the other side of the river, when they heard the sounds of battle coming from further ahead. Another few moments brought them in sight of the fighting which had started fresh since they had first left. The Yue infantry had pushed their way across the river and were now engaged with the Chu infantry stationed on the other side. Most still stood in the river, swinging away at the men on the banks with their dagger-axes and swords, but a few had broken through the line to get onto the bank. So far the men of Chu were doing a good job holding them off, but there were thousands more still assembling on the opposing bank. Wu knew that it would be nearly impossible to hold them back once they charged across the shallow water.

They went further up past the third division and were soon behind the fourth. These men were fighting on two sides. The men had managed to form up into a wedge so they could simultaneously make a stand against the chariots coming down on them from the north and the infantry coming at them from across the river. The few dozen chariots that still remained helped as best they could, mainly rushing about to draw off the enemy chariots, but there numbers were too few to make any real difference.

Dao spun the chariot around in a circle and brought it to a stop well behind the line of fighting. He stared hard at the battle taking place on two sides then glanced up at the hills behind them.

"The archers are still doing well," he said so quietly

that Wu had to strain to hear him over the clash of steel. He turned suddenly to look at Wu. "We won't stand a chance here for long if we don't take some drastic measures, and soon."

Wu's eyes narrowed and he knitted his brows. "What do you have in mind, Sire?"

"I want you to get up that hill. Locate King Yi down there in all that chaos. He must be across the river directing his troops from some safe vantage."

"And if we find him, then what?"

"Then we kill him."

Wu stared at Dao for another moment, but the Duke's attention was already back on the battle. Wu didn't think it was much of a plan, but he had to admit that he couldn't think of anything worse at the moment. It was obvious that they would be finished within the hour unless their main force arrived, but that seemed less and less likely with each minute that passed. With a shrug Wu jumped from the car and started to rush up the hill.

Rocks scattered and tumbled down behind him as he went up, and several times he stumbled and only barely stopped himself from falling completely by throwing his hands out in front of himself. After a time he started to use his arms as well as his legs to propel him up the steep incline. The sounds of the fighting diminished the further he went up, but they did not go away entirely. A few stolen glances over his shoulder was all it took to remind him of how dire their situation was.

After several minutes, his fingers bloodied in from the jagged rocks, he reached the first of the archers. The men had spotted him several minutes before, but they were so intent on loading and reloading their bows that they paid him scant attention.

"Where's the officer in charge?" Wu shouted at the first group he came upon.

One of the men, his bow drawn up to his face as he

took aim on some distant target below, cocked his head slightly behind him and to the left.

Wu scrambled on, moving around large rocks and boulders that dotted the hillside. Other groups of archers gave the same directions as the first, and finally after several minutes he asked one group where the officer was and a man had said that he was in charge.

"Duke Dao wants to know where King Yi is," Wu said panting, the sweat pouring down his face and into his already soaked robes.

"That's easy," the man said, pointing out onto the plain below. "He's in the middle of that large circle of men behind the infantry and just out of range."

Wu put his hand to his forehead to block the sun's glare and narrowed his eyes. There was a circle of chariots drawn up, several more men standing about in a wider circle. It appeared to be the seat of command, that was for sure, but Wu couldn't make out King Yi.

"Are you sure Yi's in that group?"

"Can't you see him?" the man asked. "He's got the bright blue robes on. We watched when that group came to a stop there, and the first thing that happened was a new set of robes was brought out for that man to change into. Seems their king doesn't like to spend too long in dusty clothes," the officer finished with a laugh.

Wu could make him out now, the bright blue gave him away easily, and he was surprised he hadn't noticed before. It was hard to make out, but Wu was sure that the other men around him were getting orders which they then relayed to the men on foot around them, who then went rushing off down the line of battle. Looking down on them Wu realized that Dao's plan of killing the King wasn't so far-fetched after all. There were few men guarding him, and most of the infantry was occupied with fighting their way across the river. The majority of chariots that the King possessed were buffeting the mouth of the river, while the archers that had been scattered by Min's charge were still trying to get reorganized further up the range of hills.

"Sir," Wu said to the man, "gather together your best marksmen and send them down the hills to the right flank of the infantry line. Have them wait there for further instructions."

The man's eyes narrowed. "What's going on? Are you truly meaning to strike against the King?"

"You'll be the first to see it if we do," Wu said as he turned and began hopping down the hillside.

FIFTEEN

Rocks scattered all about as Wu hopped and slid down the hill, and in just a minute he was behind the infantry lines once again. Putting his arms on his knees he bent over to catch his breath and peered about, looking for Min or Dao. After a few moments he spotted the Duke, riding up and down the line of men, shouting orders for where to firm up and get ready for the assault that was already coming at them from across the river. Wu straightened up and rushed to the chariot, hoping that it wouldn't dash off suddenly.

Another man in the car spotted Wu rushing up and clapped Dao on the shoulder. The Duke nodded when he caught sight of Wu and turned the chariot toward him.

"Well, what did you find out, Wu?"

"King Yi is in a tight circle of men and chariots just behind the infantry. It's nearly a straight line from the mouth of the river to his location."

Dao nodded. "How many men does he have guarding him?"

"No more than twenty afoot with another twenty in the chariots."

Wu gestured back up toward the hills. "I told the officer in charge to gather together his best marksmen and send them down to the end of our line."

"Good," Dao said before turning to the man next to him. "Rush to the mouth of the river and tell General Min to spare as many chariots as he can. Tell him we have fighting on the right flank."

The man nodded, hopped from the car, and sped off north. Wu climbed up into the car.

"*Is* there fighting on the right flank? I didn't see any?"

"It wouldn't do to tell Min that I mean to lead a charge against King Yi."

"It wouldn't do to lie to him either."

Dao shrugged. "By the time those chariots get here there *will* be fighting on the right flank."

Wu glanced further down the line. The Duke was right; already Yue infantry were massing heavily across the river, ready to storm across against the Chu fourth division.

"We'll have to get over the river to the south, where it comes through the mountains," Wu said, turning his attention back to Dao.

"I realize that. The fighting at the mouth of the river is too fierce; we'd never be able to break through it undetected."

"And how do you plan on getting a dozen chariots across the river?"

"There're shallow spots," Dao answered.

Wu nodded. They would tackle that problem when they got to it. "The camp should provide enough cover to get out behind their lines unseen."

"Exactly. That camp is nearly a mile long and no one in the Yue Army will be looking at it."

"And then what?" Wu asked. "We just charge at Yi and hope that we kill him."

Dao looked hard at Wu and with not a trace of doubt on his face. "Yes."

Wu only nodded, surprised at how the battle had hardened his ruler. He'd never seen Dao so serious before, nor so determined. It was as if all of his frustrations over what had befallen the once powerful State of Chu were coming to a boil under the hot sun and the unmerciful heat of the desert plain around them. For the first time since the battle started Wu felt that they *would* prevail.

The archers began arriving down from the hills just as the first chariots came down from further up the river. As ordered, Min had sent down a dozen of the chariots, a third of his force. Their absence would make protecting the left flank all the more difficult, but Wu knew that if Dao's plan succeeded, if King Yi was somehow killed in their risky charge, it could well spell the end of the battle. There were more archers than there were chariots, so Dao quickly yelled out for the best to take up positions on the chariots. There was room for only two men and a driver in each car, so by the time the men had separated themselves out there were thirty-six men total on their twelve chariots. Duke Dao and Wu were in the lead, with another archer named Po, the commander of the small battalion down from the hills.

"Gather round," Dao yelled when the cars were full, and the drivers moved about them in a circle. "We'll be heading south, looking for a shallow spot to cross the river. I mean to come around behind and circle around our camp then charge up the plain at the unprotected rear of the Yue forces. King Yi has been spotted commanding from a ring of chariots with no more men guarding him than we have here. If we do this right we'll have a chance of ending the battle." He paused to look at each of the men in the chariots around him. "Either King Yi or I will die this afternoon. I mean for it to be him. Help me make that possible."

The men nodded solemnly, for the speech was not one to cheer for. Each man knew the risks of moving behind an enemy force that numbered in the tens of thousands, completely cut off from their own forces by that enemy, a vast plain, and an un-fordable river. Even if they did manage to kill King Yi they would still have to somehow make it back across their own lines, a difficult undertaking given that most of the enemy would surely have spotted them by that time. And even getting to Yi would be difficult: there were still plenty of chariots left to the Yue forces, chariots which could easily turn away from their assault of the river's mouth and back to the rear of their lines. But possibly most worrisome to the men, considering that the majority riding out with Dao were marksmen, were the enemy archers. The largely untouched force still numbered nearly two thousand and stood in a large block just behind the infantry. A single volley from them could spell the end of their charge before it even had a chance to begin.

Without another word Dao cracked the reins hard across the two horses and sent their chariot moving, the other chariots quickly making way, their circle coming apart as each car fell into line. They raced along the river and away from the sounds of fighting and after a minute Wu glanced over his shoulder to see that they were already out of view of the battle raging behind them.

For several minutes they raced south along the river, the archers in the chariots behind them keeping a sharp look out with their keen eyes for any spot on the river that would allow their chariots to cross without difficulty. After several more minutes Wu urged Dao to slow their chariot and to wave on several of the cars behind them. It was obvious that their small force would have to move more slowly and with greater spaces between them if they were to locate a suitable crossing. It wasn't until three-quarters of an hour had elapsed that a shout came from further up their column and the other chariots raced to the stopped car.

"There!" an archer pointed excitedly. "See the swirls in the water? This spot is shallow enough across the whole length."

Already a man was halfway across the river, the water reaching no higher than the top of his ankles. Wu narrowed his eyes and after a moment saw what the man was pointing at. The water swirled and eddied all along a jagged line of the river, something that could only occur with rocks close to the surface. While he was still looking the first chariot drove into the river, slowly at first, but with greater speed once it became obvious that it wouldn't sink under the rushing water. Halfway across the man standing in the water jumped into the car and after another few moments the car was on the other side of the river, the men eagerly waving back at them.

"We cross here," Dao called out loudly before he cracked the reins and sent their chariot into the water. The river bottom was uneven and the rocks beneath them shifted under their weight, but within moments they were halfway then approaching the opposite shore. When they were safely out of the river Wu looked behind to see a line of chariots following them across. Within minutes their whole column was again racing along the river, this time on the opposite bank and toward the fighting.

What took them the better part of an hour took them less than ten minutes to cover as their chariots sped back to the sounds of battle, the fine red dust of the plain swirling up in clouds behind them. The ring of steel on steel and the shouts and cries of men fighting and dying carried to them, and Dao cracked the reins again and again to bring them to it. The hills on the other side of the river slowly turned north and eventually they were able to see the battle. The sight Wu had been dreading, Yue infantry across the river, their smaller force surrounded and greatly outnumbered, was not the sight that confronted them.

Instead, and much to his surprise, what he saw was the Yue infantry falling back from the river.

"They're falling back!" Dao yelled over the roar of their wheels as he too saw what has happening.

Wu put his hand up to his eyes to block the sun, then pulled his head back, his eyes going wide with surprise.

"Our forces have arrived from the north!" he shouted. "They've come right down on top of the Yue chariots at the river's mouth."

"And their infantry is rushing to meet the new threat," Dao said, referring to the Yue forces rushing back across the river.

"The battle is won, Sire," Wu said into Dao's ear.

"Not yet it isn't, not with King Yi still on the field."

Wu had expected that reply, but was still unhappy to hear it. "Sire, we don't have to make this reckless charge. King Yi will have no choice but to pull back now that we match or even outnumber his own forces. Already his chariots are trapped between our infantry and newly arrived chariots. Don't put yourself in needless danger."

"The battle ends here and now, Wu," Dao replied so quietly that Wu barely heard him.

Wu frowned but and gritted his teeth. There was not much he could do, he realized, so he patted Po on the arm.

"Get ready," he said to the archer.

Po nodded and thrust his bow over his head. Wu glanced back to see the other archers in the chariots behind them ready their own bows while beside him Po nocked an arrow. They would have to pull up somewhere and stop if they wanted their shots to have any chance of success; firing from moving chariots was difficult for even the most skilled, and it wouldn't do to have the element of surprise go with a reckless volley. Dao didn't seem to think so, however, for he continued to race north, even when King Yi's small command was spotted, his officers and guards obviously in confusion with the turn the battle had taken.

"Sire, we have to stop!" Wu yelled out.

Dao either didn't hear him or ignored him, for he cracked the reins once then twice, giving them a greater burst of speed. He raised his other arm up in the air and threw it forward in the motion to charge. Wu looked forward and saw that several of the men around Yi were frantically pointing toward them but before he could voice any more concerns Po angled his bow higher and let loose. His arrow was joined by dozens of others from behind, each of them sailing up and out over the hundred yards that separated them from Yi's men. The metal heads glinted in the sun as the shafts rose and then fell, all falling either short or to the side of where Yi's men were. Their element of surprise gone, they had no other choice but to continue the charge; by the time they pulled up to turn about Yi's own men would be firing down on them.

Even before his arrow was falling toward the ground Po had another nocked and he let that one fly. The other men behind them did the same, and this time a few found their marks, sending four of Yi's men to the ground dead while two others clutched at shafts sprouting from their legs. Surprise was gone, however, and Yi's men were already in a circular formation, their King at their center and heavily guarded with shields to stop any arrows that might find him.

After the second volley came the third, with much the same results, and then they were just a few dozen yards away. Wu grabbed the sword hanging from his belt and braced himself. Dao gave no sign of slowing the chariot or of turning it, and if he did neither they would slam right into the ring of horses and chariots surrounding Yi.

As they came within ten yards of the circle of men Dao let out a savage yell, dropped the reins from his hands, grabbed hold of his sword with one hand and clutched at the side of the car with the other. Wu did the same, but Po, an arrow nocked and ready, kept careful aim, either oblivious of the impact to come or totally unconcerned. When they were just yards away and Wu could see the fear in the Yue soldiers' eyes, Po let loose, his arrow slamming into and then out of the chest of the soldier directly in front of him. The last thing Wu saw was the man's eyes go wide before their horses reared and their chariot slammed into King Yi's line. After that everything went black.

SIXTEEN

When Wu came to he was lying on the ground, his sword still clutched tightly in his hand. All around him were the sounds of battle; of steel ringing and men and horses yelling and screaming and dying. He sat up, his head swimming. The first thing he saw was an overturned chariot still fastened to two horses, one dead the other dying loudly and painfully. There was no sign of either Po or Dao, however, and a quick look around confirmed that neither was lying about dead, at least not within his narrow field of view. It looked as though most of the dozen chariots had followed Dao's charge right up to the end, for chariots were piled about, overturned and in some cases atop one another, their horses contorted into all sorts of gruesome poses, many already dead but most screaming out in agony.

Wu pushed himself to his feet with his free hand and was able to see over some of the wrecked chariots. All about him men were fighting, most hand-to-hand with swords, although a few hung back and took aim with their bows. He turned about and realized that he had been facing away from where they had charged. In front of him sat Po's lifeless body, impaled on a jagged splinter of wood from one of the ruined chariots, his eyes wide and blood already drying in a thin line from his mouth. There was no way the archer could have survive the crash, Wu knew that when they were still in the chariot, for the last shot had cost him all. Duke Dao, however, had grasped onto the chariot as Wu had, and he could still be alive, perhaps fighting even now.

The first step that Wu took was agony and his face grimaced up in pain, his body almost toppling back to the ground. He quickly steadied himself, his arms bracing his leg, and looked down. There was no discernable wound and after pulling up his robes he could only see a large bruise, bright red but already turning a purplish black. A bone could be broken, he thought, but he was able to put some weight on it, so the injury couldn't be too severe. Gingerly he took a step forward, and then another. His leg sent shooting pains all throughout his body, but he gritted his teeth and carried on. Several steps brought him to Po's body, and from there he could see past the first line of wrecked chariots.

What he saw was pure chaos. Men bloodied from the charge were standing about, some barely managing that, and swinging away at one another with swords. Many had trouble keeping their balance, and swayed this way and that with each swing, often staggering past their opponents when an attack missed. The sight would have been comical had the circumstances not been so serious. We peered about, past the dozen men fighting away at one another, but couldn't see Dao. Gripping his sword tightly at his side he limped out from behind the line of ruined chariots and steered his way around the men engaged in their struggles. He managed to move quickly, his part-run part-hop movements taking him past the battling men and to the second line of chariots, a line of King Yi's that were undamaged and with many of the horses still tied to them. The sounds of more fighting and yelling were coming from the other side as Wu craned his head around one of the large cars.

On the other side he saw men fighting, and judging from their performance, they were the men in the rear of the charge on his side and the closest to King Yi on the Yue side. They swung at one another expertly with their swords, the ring of steel echoing out loudly. Most likely these men had rushed up to the undamaged chariots, past men that were laying about after the initial impact, men they had suspected were dead, or else simply too bruised and battered to offer a fight. They had obviously met the main guard of King Yi and were now battling it out. But still there was no sight of Duke Dao.

And then he heard it, a cry for help coming from the other side of the chariot.

Wu limped out further and saw King Yi down on one knee, blood coming from his left side. Duke Dao stood over him, his sword bloodied and swinging down for another strike. Yi managed to get his own blade up in time to block the swing, and shouted out again. Several of the Yue men battling looked over, but none of them was in a position to break off their own fight and get to their king in time. Wu knew that it wouldn't be long, however, before someone heard the king's cries and came to his aid. Dao seemed to sense it too, for his sword came back up and down again quickly, ringing against Yi's blade as the king blocked the attack. Yi tried to rise up, but it was obvious the wound in his side was serious. Wu limped out from the chariot and toward Dao, hoping to get to his side in time to end the fight with the king and get him safely to one of the still-undamaged chariots and then back to their own lines.

He was just a few yards from the two rulers when an arrow slammed into Dao's back. The force of it caused Dao's arms to splay out in front of him, but only for a moment before he regained his balance. Wu turned

about to see an archer behind him, standing next to
the same chariot he'd just come from. The man was
already nocking another arrow to his bow and would
be ready to fire in moments. Wu glanced back at Dao
and saw that he was preparing another swing at Yi,
despite the arrow sticking from him. Without thinking
of the risk or the pain in his leg, Wu broke into as
much of a run as he could manage and charged at the
archer. The man had his bow up and was about to
loose his arrow at Wu, his eyes suddenly going wide at
the sight of the wounded man rushing at him, when
Wu threw his sword. The blade spun end-over-end
and hit the man, striking his bow first and sending the
arrow skittering to the ground. Wu was on him in the
next moment, pummeling him with his fists. The
archer fought back and Wu saw him reach for a dagger
at his belt. Wu punched him again and again and the
man's hands moved away from the dagger and to his
face. Wu reached for the dagger, pulled it free, and
drove it into the man's chest. The man let out a
guttural moan, but Wu didn't wait to see if he was
dead. He spun about to look back at Dao and Yi, and
his eyes went wide.

"No!" he cried out.

Dao was now the one on his knees, his sword held
loosely in his hand, its point resting on the ground. Yi
was standing over him, his own sword now bloodied.
The king looked up when he heard the cry, and smiled
at the sight of Wu staring back at him. Yi grasped his
sword with both hands in an overhand grip and drove
the point down into Dao's chest, pulling it out again
quickly. Dao fell to the ground face forward and didn't
move. Yi stared back at Wu, the same smile on his
face, and was about to start toward him when one of
his men rushed up to him and began shouting at him
while pulling him back. Yi started to argue, his eyes
still on Wu, but the man was insistent. He pointed
behind Wu, pleading with Yi, and whatever he said

must have convinced him. The king nodded, smiled one last time at Wu, and then let the man pull him away and out of sight. Men were still fighting, but there were only a few, and the sight of Duke Dao laying face down on the ground seemed to give the Chu soldiers a boost. They quickly dispatched the last of their opponents, a few rushing toward where King Yi had been pulled away to, others going to their fallen Duke. Wu struggled to his feet and limped to his fallen ruler. The other Chu soldiers had already turned him over onto his back, and his eyes were still open and peering about when Wu got to him.

"Sire!" Wu said as he pushed his way past the few men staring down at their duke.

"Wu," Dao said so quietly that Wu had to bend down to within inches of his face. "Did you see? I had him finished, I-"

Dao coughed and a bloody-red phlegm came up onto his face.

"Sire, don't speak."

Dao struggled through the coughing fit, more blood coming up, before he was once again able to talk.

"I ran him...clean through...his side....bloodied."

"I know, Sire, I saw." Wu had to choke back tears at the sight of Dao struggling to speak.

"That...cursed archer..."

"I killed him," Wu said, and a slight smile came to Dao's face.

"And we'll finish off Yi as well, you can be sure of that," Wu added.

"Good...good," Dao said.

His voice trailed off and his eyes went from Wu to the sky above. His gaze locked on whatever sight he saw and stayed that way for several moments.

"Sire?" Wu said, gently shaking Dao. "Sire!"

"He's gone," one of the men standing near said.

"May Shangdi bless him," another said.

"May Shangdi bless him," all of the men said as one.

Wu reached up and ran his hand over Dao's face, closing his eyes. He hung his head for a moment then started to push himself back to his feet, one of the soldiers grasping his arm for support.

"Help me load him into one of the undamaged chariots," Wu said when he was standing.

"They were all damaged beyond use in the charge," one of the men said.

"Then put him in one of the Yue chariots!" Wu snapped.

"Yes, sir," the man said, and four of the soldiers bent down to pick up their fallen ruler by the arms and legs. They carried him over to one of the Yue chariots and laid him down inside the car. One of the men pulled his robes up over his head and laid them over Dao's body, unconcerned with his nakedness. Wu limped behind them and climbed up into the car, careful not to step on Dao's body, and took up the reins.

"Take another chariot to the river," Wu said to the soldiers staring up at him. "Tell General Min what has happened. Tell him that I'll be heading south along the river, back to the capital. Bring another chariot; I won't have the Duke's body ride into the capital aboard a chariot from the State of Yue."

The men bowed their heads as Wu stared into each of their faces, none saying a word. Wu nodded at them and then snapped the reins, steering the two horses around the carnage of wrecked chariots and dead men and horses. Within moments he was out of the area of battle and onto the open plain once again. A quick glance up toward the fighting revealed that the Yue forces were in full retreat, rushing north up the plain from the direction they'd come, the Chu soldiers fast on their heels. The battle was won, but Min was not letting the enemy escape. He meant to finish King Yi and the State of Yue, here on the vast plain if possible, outside of the gates of Shouchun if not. Wu doubted those plans would change once word of Dao's death reached him; most likely it would only embolden him and the soldiers, ending the State of Yue all the quicker. *But at what price?* Wu thought Duke Dao's death would embolden the soldiers to fight harder, but would it also embolden the Chu nobles to fight as well? There discontent at the changes Wu had brought had been checked by Dao, but would that discontent stay in check when Dao's son Su Xiong took power? The nobles may well strike out against the young man as soon as word got back to Ying of the duke's death. The thought made Wu crack the reins all the harder, the better to get back to the capital with the Duke's body before word did.

Wu was racing along the river when he heard shouts behind him. He turned and saw a dozen chariots several yards back and on the opposite bank. In the lead chariot, waving frantically and shouting to get his attention, was Min. Wu reined up and brought his chariot to a stop. Within moments the other chariots had come to rest across the river and Min and a dozen men wasted no time walking right into and across the water.

Min was the first one up the bank and he didn't even look at Wu as he walked around the chariot and to Dao's body. He pulled the robes away and stared down for several moments without saying a word. The other soldiers walked up behind him and after a minute Min pulled the robes back up over Dao's head.

"How did it happen?" Min said, turning at last to face Wu, his face tired and weary from the battle, and now full of sorrow over his dead ruler.

"The Duke had the reins and led the charge himself," Wu began. "He slammed right into the line of chariots guarding Yi. I was thrown from the car and lost consciousness, and when I came to Dao was nowhere in sight. I staggered about, eventually coming upon him and Yi. Dao was standing over the wounded king, when an arrow took him in the back. I killed the archer, but the damage was done: King Yi finished Dao."

"And you let him get away?" Min's eyes bore into him accusingly.

"Perhaps a dozen of the men still standing went after him, the rest after we got the Duke's body loaded into a chariot."

"I see," Min said slowly as he turned to look back across the river. He folded his arms in front of him and remained quiet for several moments as he thought. "It won't do to bring back the Duke of Chu in a Yue chariot," he said at last, turning to face Wu once again. "We'll carry him across the river and you can load him into my own car."

Min walked to Dao's body and began pulling it from the chariot, several of the soldiers coming up to help. Within moments they had the body hoisted up over their heads and were heading into the waist-deep water. Wu followed behind them in silence. When they reached the opposite bank they placed the body in the chariot and Min turned to Wu.

"I'll provide you with an escort of chariots to see you to Ying. I cannot spare these men here, but I will have others sent back this way. They'll catch up with you on the road."

Wu nodded. "And you? Are you going to chase Yi all the way to Shouchun?"

"If that's what it takes," Min said solemnly. "When our forces arrived from the north they slammed into Yue's rear, taking out the majority of the archers. The chariots continued right into the lines of infantry, cutting hundreds down before the men could reorganize themselves, and then all they could do was make an orderly retreat. If the wound you say King Yi had is grave, then perhaps he'll not be leading the remnants of his army for long."

"I'll come back to Ying as quickly as I can, but not

until Yue is dealt with," Min continued. "Su will no doubt insist upon a quick, though lavish, funeral for his father."

"Shangdi demands such," Wu said.

Min nodded. "He does. You'll both understand my not being there, then?"

"Come back to the capital as fast as you can," Wu said. "I fear for Su. The nobles will see this as an opportunity for themselves. We may have won the battle, and we may even defeat the State of Yue for good, but we've lost our duke. Word of the Duke's death may even reach the capital before I do, and if that's the case many of the nobles will come rushing back."

"Handle them as best as you can, I'll make haste in dealing with Yi. If everything goes right he'll not see his own capital again."

Wu nodded and he and Min clasped hands before Wu got into the chariot with Dao's body. He took up the reins and Min gave a final wave from his own chariot before putting it into motion. Within minutes he was out of view. Once again Wu was alone with Dao's body. He looked down at the blood-stained brown robes covering the duke and thought of the man he had come to know so well over the past two years. When he had met him, Dao had been more timid than anything. Oh, he was a ruler, able to be strong when necessary, but he had lacked the decisiveness that was needed if Chu wanted to again become great. That trait which had been lacking when they first met had been in evidence on the battlefield today, however, and it had cost Dao his life. Hopefully his death would not be in vain, and his courage at the end would be a signal for his son on how to rule. Wu let out a deep breath and cracked the reins across the two horses. He had to get back to Ying, and fast.

SEVENTEEN

Pai Fen burst into the room, a servant close behind.

"Sir, you can't go in there," the servant said futilely to his back.

Pai rushed up to the desk, a piece of paper clutched tightly in his hand, a large smile on his face. Dao An looked up at the face he had come to know so well over the years in the Noble's Council and raised his hand.

"It's alright, leave us," Dao said to his servant with a dismissive wave.

It wasn't until the servant had closed the large double doors that Pai backed away from the desk and began pacing the room excitedly.

"Well, what is it that's so important you have to barge in here like this," Dao said, his annoyance at the sudden intrusion outweighed by his curiosity.

Pai held up the paper in front of him and thrust it out to Dao. Dao took it gingerly and carefully smoothed it out on his desk, but Pai didn't give him the chance to read it.

"Duke Dao is dead!" he cried out in joyous relief.

Dao An looked up at him, his eyes narrowing, not sure if Pai was out of his senses or actually telling the truth. He quickly scanned the paper in front of him. It detailed the battle that had taken place on a vast plain two day's march from the city, but it was the last words that stopped Dao short. 'Duke Dao was killed in a charge against King Yi,' it said simply.

"'Duke Dao was killed,'" Dao read aloud from the letter, his face screwed up in disbelief.

"In a charge against King Yi, if you can believe that!" Pai said loudly and with a smile. "Who would have thought that our timid duke, so fond of sitting in his palace on cushions and lace, could find it in himself to lead a charge in battle."

"And against King Yi of all people," Dao said quietly, rising from his chair to peer out the window and down to the street below. Peasants walked about with sacks of grain, baskets of produce, and animals in cages or under arms. None were aware of the enormity of what had just taken place a two-day ride from the city.

Dao turned urgently back to Pai. "When did this arrive? How old is the news?"

"Not an hour ago," Pai replied. "As to how old," he scratched at his gray mustache and beard, "that is not as easy to say. I suspect the battle took place yesterday. This message is from one of the smaller towns on the road leading to the plain where it took place."

"And who is the one who sent it?" Dao asked. "How many others know?"

"One of the lesser nobles that was sent out of the capital during the first wave of Wu's exiles," Pai answered. "As you know, I've taken great pains to have a loyal network of such men, eyes and ears around the state, if you will."

"Yes." Dao knew all about Pai's network of eyes and ears, men's whose allegiance ran toward Pai and his money, not to the State of Chu.

"As to your other question 'how many others know,' that I cannot be certain of. You know quickly news can spread when nobles begin to talk. Thankfully it's confined to the countryside for now."

"We'd best find out, and fast," Dao said. "If this battle took place yesterday then the Duke's body will be arriving at the head of the army tomorrow."

Dao began rustling through papers on his desk, overturning an inkpot in the process, before he looked up to see Pai staring at him with that smile so many found ingratiating but which Dao now only found annoying.

"What aren't you telling me?" Dao said quickly.

"The Duke's body will not be coming back into the city at the head of the army," Pai laughed. "It will be coming back with an escort of but a dozen chariots."

"A dozen chariots?" Dao's confusion must have been plain, for Pai pulled out one of the chairs and sat down across from the desk.

"General Min has gone in pursuit of King Yi's army. It's said that the King suffered a grievous injury during the battle, by Duke Dao's own hand." Pai's smile got larger as he spoke, and his eyes gleamed when he came to the last. "It's also said that Wu Qi drives the chariot that holds the duke's body."

"No!" Dao said, falling back into his own chair. "Shangdi be praised!"

"Shangdi be praised!" Pai echoed, rising from his chair with a laugh and few quick hops about the room.

Dao leaned back in his chair. The army would not be back in time for the funeral, not if they were going off to finish King Yi. They might even have to go all the way to Shouchun; perhaps even engage in a lengthy siege. Tradition dictated that the Duke be given a funeral within two days of his death, and that would be tomorrow.

"There will be no protection for Wu Qi when he arrives," Dao said.

"Few soldiers remain in the city," Pai agreed. "Now is our time to act."

"Wu Qi is not a stupid man. He'll suspect some kind of plot against him."

"Let him jump at shadows," Pai said. "We control the city, there's no way he can stop us."

"And what of the Duke's son? Su will be Duke in his own right now."

"He is a young man, and even more pliable than his father was. He will go along with whatever we want, he has to."

"You sound quite sure of yourself."

Pai sat back down across from Dao. "Nobles across the country are already receiving the news from their own contacts. Many are already returning from the nearest cities. By this time tomorrow a hundred of them will be in attendance for the funeral. They'll bring their men with them, men trained as soldiers; men who serve us, not Su." Pai folded his hands in front of his face and peered over them at Dao. "Perhaps it's time for a new ruler of Chu, one not of the Xiong line."

"That is a dangerous route to take, and one that not all the nobles will be so quick to follow."

"Many will follow it if it means they can return to the capital. If it's Fei Lin that you're worried about, don't be; he's already agreed to whatever course I deem prudent," Pai said.

"You spoke to him before coming to me?" Dao said, perturbed.

"I knew that you would go along with me, I didn't know if Fei would. It seemed wise to find out where he stood before we put a plan into place."

"You should have come to me first," Dao said.

Pai waved the words away. "It is done, Fei is with us."

Dao rose once again and went to the window. He looked down on the people going about their business, oblivious to the plots hatching around them.

"And what is this plan?" Dao asked. Even without taking his eyes from the window he knew that Pai was smiling.

EIGHTEEN

Wu was met by fifty chariots when he was still an hour outside Anyi. Word had obviously gotten back to the capital about the duke's death, something he had hoped wouldn't have happened. It had been a foolish hope, he had known that the moment it entered his head, but he had hoped it nonetheless. The men were wearing white robes, funeral garb, and in the lead chariot rode Su Xiong, the man who would soon be the new Duke of Chu. The long white sleeves of his robes billowed in the wind and his long black hair flew behind him, untied. The young man, Wu still had trouble not thinking of him as still a boy, was clean shaven, and even from a distance of several dozen yards Wu could make out the piercing black eyes that looked so commanding, but which merely hid his timidity.

Wu raised one arm up as he tugged on the reins with the other, a signal for the chariots behind him to slow to a stop. Su Xiong did the same at the head of his column, but kept his own chariot moving until it came up alongside Wu.

"Wu Qi," Su said as he handed his reins to the soldier next to him and hopped down from the chariot, "thank you for making haste from the battlefield."

"It was the least I could do, Sire," Wu said honestly.

Su walked around to the back of Wu's chariot just as Wu jumped down. "I'm not your Duke yet, not until we have the funeral for my father."

Wu nodded, but Su didn't see; his eyes were fastened on the covered body on the floor of the chariot's car. He stared at it for several moments as if getting up his courage to have a look, then finally stepped forward and threw off the brown robes, now more covered in dust than blood. Duke Dao's body had become quite pale over the past day, but the dry and crusted blood that covered his chest and side made it clear how he had died.

"I hear that he died fighting King Yi, and almost had him too, until an archer interfered."

"He had the King on his knees," Wu confirmed. "I killed the archer myself, but not until he had already put an arrow in your father's back."

"And my father ordered the charge?" Su asked as he replaced the robes over his father's face. "He was never one known for his courage and daring."

"It was his idea and there was no talking him out of it; I tried," Wu replied.

"If he only would have waited another hour the northern force would have arrived," Su said more to himself than to Wu.

Wu nodded again, surprised by how much the events of the battle had already filtered back to the capital. Wu had raced back well into the night, stopping only when it became impossible to see, and then starting again well before the sun was up. How had news traveled so fast? Someone in the army must have sent off a bird to Su, he thought. And if a bird could have gone to the duke's heir, how many had been sent to his enemies? What did the nobles know, and what were they planning on doing next? Wu left the questions unsaid and inquired about the funeral instead.

"We'll head straight to the temple," Su said. "Arrangements are in place and hundreds are already awaiting us there. The news of my father's death came as quite a shock to most, so we can expect thousands to line the route to the temple. They were already gathering when we left." Su raised his arm up and waved back at his column of men. Several jumped down from their chariots and rushed toward him.

"Hundreds?" Wu asked, surprised that so many would already be in the large temple to Shangdi. "Is that safe?"

Su's brows knitted as he looked at Wu. "Why wouldn't it be? What harm could come at a funeral for my father?"

The boy's as naïve as he is young, Wu thought as the soldiers arrived and began lifting up Dao's body. "The Nobles, Sire. Surely some of them view this time, when the old duke is dead and the new one yet to be proclaimed, as the perfect opportunity to end the Xiong line for good. Such an act would throw the city into chaos, and a strong noble, Pai Fen or Dao An for example, would welcome such as an excuse to seize power."

"It's funny that you should mention those two, Wu, for it was both of them together that brought me the news of the battle." Su clasped his hands behind his back and followed the soldiers carrying his father's body toward his own chariot. The soldiers gently placed the body on the floor of the chariot then rushed back to their own cars. Su turned again to face Wu when they were gone. "I would have expected my father's generals to send word of the battle, and my father's death, as quickly as possible. Instead that word was sent through others, and to the nobles, not the duke's son."

"General Min and I both thought that secrecy would be the best course to take," Wu explained. "Both of us fear what the nobles are capable of, especially those two." Wu reached out and grabbed Su's arm. "I beg you, Sire, send word back for the temple to be cleared. Let us have a small and private funeral."

Su looked down at Wu's hand on his arm and then into Wu's eyes. Wu frowned and pulled his hand back before Su climbed back into his chariot. "The enemy you should fear is defeated and running back to Shouchun as we speak," Su said as he took the reins from the soldier next to him. "The Nobles of Chu mean us no harm."

Su cracked his reins lightly and steered the horses around Wu's chariot so they were facing back toward the city. He stopped once again to look down on Wu.

"You've done much good for Chu, but you've also made many enemies along the way. My rule will not be like my father's, and I fear I've no need of a castoff from the Wei Army any longer. Your ideas have caused strife in the state and done more harm than good. We were nearly crushed on those plains, proving that your military prowess is no more. You're free to attend the funeral, then free to do as you please."

Su cracked the reins and his chariot lurched into motion. Wu stood in the faint cloud of dust thrown up and watched the next Duke of Chu ride back along the road from whence he came, his chariots falling into line behind him.

Wu watched him go, the chariots that had followed him from the battle also following Su back into the city.

What did he mean by 'my rule will not be like my father's? Wu thought as he watched the column of chariots disappear into their cloud of dust. Sure, Duke Dao hadn't been the most actionable of rulers, but he'd proven his valor at the end. And more importantly, Wu knew, he had accepted new and radical ideas. Dao had known that his state was falling further and further behind, and he took action to remedy the situation. The fact that those actions just happened to be spurred by someone from the State of Qi shouldn't have had much bearing.

But perhaps it did, after all, Wu thought. The nobles wanted him dead, Min was certain of it and Wu was himself now. Duke Dao had never been close to the nobles, knowing them for what they were: a true drain on the state. Was Su different? Had he somehow developed a cozy relationship with the nobles over the past two years? Wu hadn't spent too much time around Su, but he did sense him to be even more timid than his father had been at times. Was he now making up for that timidity with the power of the nobles backing him up? Or was he blindly setting himself up for a tragedy?

Wu hopped back into his chariot and charged toward the city. If he was in danger, Su was even more so.

NINETEEN

The Temple of Shangdi was filled to overflowing. A sea of white it seemed the temple was as nobles, soldiers, and citizens alike crammed themselves into every available space, and still more jostled to come in. The temple rose up and out from a large circular floor, three levels of tiers and balconies full of seats where people could come to watch and pray and mourn. The balconies were filled, but the floor was not. The dark marble stones shone brightly and reflected the fluttering flames of the numerous torches burning on wall sconces from all three levels. The city guard were decked out in white for the occasion, each holding a large dagger-axe on poles that stretched higher than they did. Together they'd created a circle around the large central dais where Duke Dao's body was to lay and all the way to the large double-door entrance. The dais was empty, and all in attendance looked eagerly toward the doors, waiting.

"It shouldn't be much longer now," Pai Fen said to Dao An on his left. "Su Xiong has already entered the city."

"And Wu Qi?" Dao asked.

"Following behind Su. Both should be here."

"Let us hope so," Fei Lin said. The Daoist had

traded his simple brown robes for even simpler white for the occasion. "Your plan will be for naught otherwise."

"He'll be here," Pai said.

The Hall was filled with the quite hum of hushed conversation. Nobles made up a large portion of the crowd, but not as large as they once would have before Wu Qi's reforms sent most of them from the capital. Still, many had made the journey once they had learned of their duke's death, and they numbered near two hundred. An even larger group was the various bureaucrats of the city. Two days of mourning had been declared once word had gotten back of the battle, and all government offices had been closed. Many came to pay their respects to the man they had once worked for, but more had come thinking their attendance would further their advancement in whichever department they served. By far the largest group, however, were common citizens and peasants. Only those wearing white had been allowed into the Hall, but the common people had never been known for their cleanliness; their robes were more often faded and even stained, giving the shifting sea of people on the lower level and ground floor a motley appearance of spoiled milk and even worse. Still, none could doubt their devotion, and of the hundreds in the Hall, only they had eyes stained with tears.

For every one person in attendance in the Hall there were five people clamoring outside. The streets around the temple teemed with people, most from the cities, but many from the surrounding towns and villages. Hundreds had begun lining the funeral route the day before, their only hope being to catch a glimpse of their fallen ruler's body as it entered the temple. Their voices were loud, and even the thick wooden walls of the temple could not keep the sounds at bay.

Those sounds suddenly stopped, a palpable thing that all inside noticed at once, and which could only mean one thing: Duke Dao had arrived. Several minutes of tense silence followed as all conversations ceased. All in the Hall peered down anxiously at the Temple's entrance.

Suddenly the doors were thrown open, and all within could see that it had started raining outside, something none of them had noticed over the hum within and cacophony without. The white-robed city guards lifted and then slammed the butts of their dagger-axes onto the marble floor, once, twice, then three times, the sound deafening in the cavernous temple, and the silence that followed even more so.

"It begins," Pai whispered to the two men beside him.

TWENTY

Wu was thankful that the long line of chariots had separated into two columns before they came to a stop, leaving the street empty between them. He cracked the reins to give his horses and extra burst of speed and was soon rushing between them; the dozen chariots that had ridden with him from the battlefield still close behind. Ahead loomed the large three-tiered Temple of Shangdi, one of the tallest structures in that area of the city. Wu had walked by it many times, even stopping to gaze up at it in thought for hours at a time when he had first arrived in the city, but on this day he gave it's beauty little thought. Inside hundreds waited to mourn their ruler, but he knew that several might have different ideas.

He reached the end of the line of chariots and pulled to a stop still several dozen yards from the temple. Su Xiong's chariot had stopped close to the doors and he could see several soldiers and Su himself lifting Duke Dao's body up out of the chariot and onto a white-draped carrying platform. Su took the lead position and he and five other men hoisted the platform up onto their shoulders and disappeared inside the temple. Wu handed the reins to the soldier next to him and hopped off of the chariot. He glanced down at his sword laying on the floor of the car, but shook his head. It would be out of place to bring a weapon into the temple, even if some were already there in his enemy's hands. Several of the soldiers that had accompanied him from the battlefield fell in behind him and he nodded back at them as he walked toward the Temple entrance. They represented the men that had fought and died with Duke Dao; they deserved a place at the funeral.

No one tried to stop them as they made their way toward the doors. White-clad city guards held back the crowd, although most of the citizens and peasants in attendance just looked on with blank faces and tears in their eyes. They had gotten their glimpse of their ruler's body, but still they remained.

As Wu stepped through the large double-doors he was struck by the sheer amount of people within. Hundreds filled the floor; common peasants all dressed in their best and cleanest white robes, while the balconies above held bureaucrats and nobles. The central floor was bare, however, a long line of city guards holding the people at bay, their dagger-axes reflecting the torchlight.

Ahead of him Su Xiong and the five other men were already laying Duke Dao's body onto the large central dais. The soldiers backed away when the body was down, but Su remained standing next to his father. He began reaching into his robes for something that Wu couldn't' see.

Suddenly a crossbow quarrel struck the duke's lifeless body. A few gasps came from the crowd, but most hadn't noticed, although Su did. He took a step back just as another bolt came down right where he had been standing. It clattered harmlessly off the marble floor. Many more took notice of that second bolt, and the crowded Hall erupted. The peasants on the ground level rushed the white-clad guards in their eagerness to get to the doors, and the guards could do little to hold them back. On the higher levels, too, men stood up and began rushing toward the stairs that would take them down to the sole exit from the temple. All the while more and more crossbow bolts rained down.

Wu charged toward the central dais, his eyes drawn upward into the higher levels, but he could see no one with a crossbow at hand. No doubt whoever it was had gone to great pains to conceal their weapons, but the amount of bolts raining down indicated that there had to be at least a dozen attackers.

Su's soldiers had rushed back to the dais after the first few bolts and they did their best to shield him. It would be nearly impossible to get him out of the temple with the frightened crowd rushing the doors. All they could do was sit and wait. None of them had bows or crossbows of their own, not even swords; they were helpless to make any kind of counterattack, even if they knew who it was that was attacking.

Wu punched and kicked and threw peasants out of the way in his rush to get to the dais. Thankfully the doors to the temple were tall and wide and already the floor was emptying. Most of the city guards around him had stopped trying to corral the peasants and instead began rushing toward the two staircases that led up opposite sides of the temple walls to the levels above. Men were rushing down those same stairs, however, and Wu knew that it would be several more minutes before any of them reached the second level, and several minutes more before the third, where most of the attacks were probably coming from.

The crossbow bolts continued to rain down and Wu saw several of them sprouting from Dao's lifeless body. Several more were sticking from the guards covering Su. At least one of the men that had rushed to protect the next duke was already lying on the floor dead. When Wu finally arrived at the dais, several more looked like they would quickly join him.

"Sire!" Wu called out. "Sire, we have to close the doors!"

"What!" Su's desperate voice cried out from under three of his guards. "Close the doors? We have to get *out* the doors."

"Sire, if we close the doors then the attackers will be trapped inside. We'll know who did this."

"Get me to the doors!" Su yelled in response.

"We can close the doors once the heir is safe," one of the guards said to Wu in a calmer voice.

Wu nodded. "To the doors then."

The guards rose from the floor and huddled around Su. One man quickly went down with two crossbow bolts in his back, and Wu jumped to take up his spot. They were moving quickly toward the doors, but the bolts continued to rain down. Another guard was struck, once, then twice, and then he was down. They had only gone a few more steps when another suffered the same fate. Only three guards and Wu remained and they still had two dozen yards to go before they reached the doors.

"We're almost there, we-"

Wu was cut off as a crossbow bolt slammed into the small of his back. He wrenched his arm back to pull it out when another struck him between the shoulders. He gritted his teeth in pain. Only a few more yards, he thought as his vision began to cloud. Then another bolt took him in the leg and he was somehow on his stomach on the floor. The guards left him there, the two that remained around Su, as they wrestled the next Duke of Chu toward the doors. Wu smiled slightly as he saw them reach the doors, and then he heard footsteps near his head. He tried to turn and look but another sharp pain erupted from his back and everything went black.

TWENTY-ONE

Pai Fen rushed down the stairs, taking them two at a time when he could, pushing and shoving those in his way when he couldn't. Already he was down to the first level and had but one flight remaining before he was on the ground floor. Behind him Dao An and Fei Lin cursed as they shoved past men trying to fill into the gap left in Pai's wake, so fast was he moving.

Already several of the guards around Su were down, but several more remained, and now Wu Qi was at the dais. He was gesturing frantically toward the doors, and a few moments later the guards and Su were on their feet and moving away from the unprotected and toward the safety of the doors.

Pai frowned and pushed a peasant out of his way. He had only to get down a few more stairs and he'd be on the floor. But would his crossbow men have finished their task by then? Wu Qi was still alive, as was Su. If it was guards he had wanted killed he could have done so with a much lower risk and cost. As he watched Wu Qi and the guards shuffle closer to the doors he realized that if he wanted things done right he would have to do them himself.

He jumped down the last few stairs, knocking a peasant to the ground in front of him, and looked up just in time to see Wu Qi take a bolt in the back. Another quickly followed, but still the man pushed on.

He's determined, I'll give him that much, Pai thought as he watched the man struggle to continue. He rushed out onto the floor just as another bolt struck Wu, this time in the leg. That was it, the man went down. Bolts continued to rain down on the other two guards and Su, but none were finding their mark, and Pai didn't think they would. Only a few yards separated them from the door, and unless some miracle happened they would escape. The same couldn't be said for Wu Qi, however. Pai stepped up to the man and pulled a dagger from inside his robes. Wu tried to turn his head at the sound of him, but Pai didn't give him the chance. With one quick thrust he drove the dagger down into Wu's back and saw his body shudder, then go still.

Now, if I can just get to Su, he thought. He pulled the dagger free and wiped it on Wu's robes. But it was too late, he saw; Su was already out of the temple and wet from the pouring rain. There would be other opportunities, Pai thought as he put the dagger back into his robes and rushed to the doors.

"Sire, Sire," he called as he came out into the rain. "Are you hurt?"

Su looked up at him as he came out and shook his head, still dazed. "I'm unharmed."

"Oh, praise Shangdi!" Pai shouted. "When I saw Wu go down behind you I wasn't sure you were alright."

Su's brows knitted and he looked about him. "Wu is not here?"

"He was struck several times and went down," one of the remaining guards said.

Su looked thoughtful for a few moments, then looked back up at the temple, his eyes going up its circular walls all they way to the crenellations on top.

"How many remain inside?" he asked finally.

"Many of the guards that rushed up to the higher

levels have already been shot down," one of the city guards that had been near the door when they got outside replied. "People are still swarming out of there; any of them could be one of the attackers."

"Close the doors immediately," Su said.

"Sire, is that wise?" Pai asked, too quickly he immediately realized.

Su looked him up and down, his look cold and uncompromising, and Pai felt a ball of fear lodge in his throat.

"Was it wise to call this attack?" Su asked.

Pai had no trouble looking surprised. *How could he know?*

"What do you mean, Sire?"

Su put his arm to Pai's back and began guiding him back toward the doors of the temple. "Was it me or Wu that you were after, Pai? Or did you think to take us both? You very nearly succeeded."

"Sire, you are mistaken, I would never do anything to hurt you, never dream of hurting you."

"I bet it came as quite a disappointment when you learned the General Min would not be here as well, didn't it?" Su's voice was iron.

They had reached the doors and stood before them, the flood of people trying to escape temporarily stopped by four large guards, their dagger axes blocking the way. Pai looked nervously within while Su looked hard at Pai.

"Why?" Su asked. "And tell it true, Pai. Wu warned me of you on the road, but I didn't listen. Why?"

"Sire, I never-"

Pai wasn't given a chance to finish. Su reached into his robes and pulled a dagger out in one swift motion, slamming it into Pai's chest with another. Pai reeled back, surprise on his face, then fell into the doorway, his eyes wide and lifeless. Su kicked his body clear of the doors just as Dao An and Fei Lin rushed to them.

"Sire," they both said as they looked from him to

Pai's body.

"Are you alright, Sire?" Dao asked.

Su looked at the two men hard before speaking. "How many nobles remain within?"

"More than a hundred," Fei said. "They were all on the third level, the same as where the attacks were coming from. Many are still up there trying to get down."

Su nodded then turned back to his guards, dozens more of whom now stood at his back. "Burn it."

The guards nodded and several rushed away to gather torches and pitch.

"Sire, you cannot, there are still nobles in there," Dao argued.

"I know," Su replied, "and so are you."

He pushed the two men back through the doorway and several of his guards slammed the doors shut.

"Burn it." Su said again as he walked back through his guards, the rain falling all about him. "Burn them all."

HISTORICAL NOTE

The Warring States period was a time of much bloodshed and barbarity. It might seem a bit much to have Su Xiong order all the nobles in the temple burned, and that would be correct. That was my own addition to events which actually took place.

Duke Dao was the ruler of the State of Chu, and his son was named Su. However, Dao was not a duke, but a king. I changed the titles myself because many other states had kings and it became difficult to keep track of them all, as you might have seen in the first book of the series.

Duke Dao did die, just not in battle. He ruled for twenty-one years and died in 381 BC. Duke Dao was given a funeral in the capital, and nobles did plot to assassinate him, although they weren't Pai Fen and Dao An, who are two characters from my own imagination. I tried to put what I thought all the plotting and corrupt nobles were like into those two characters. Fei Lin gets it in the end as well because he represents the Daoist influence. It was true that they cried out against the warring actions of the state which came about through Wu Qi's policy changes.

Those nobles got their wish and had bowmen in place at the funeral. Wu Qi was quick and managed to spot them. He rushed toward King Dao's body and was killed in a rain of arrows. Many struck the dead duke, which greatly angered his son, who then ordered all of the nobles involved in the plot to be executed, as well as their families.

Wu Qi was indeed a real general who lived during the Warring States period. He was actually not from the State of Qi, but the State of Wey, one of the smaller states. He did serve in the Wei Army and was appointed to rule over Xihe, the area between the Luo and Yellow Rivers that the state had recently fought and won from the State of Qin. He also was forced into exile by the ruler of the State of Wei, which was led by Marquis Wu. The two men had developed a bad relationship somehow, although the reasons for this are unclear. The story of Meilin, the woman they both loved, is my own. There were rumors at the time, however, that Wu Qi did marry a noble's daughter. The story then goes that he had her killed to make the ruler of the small State of Lu happy, which he was serving at the time.

After being exiled from the State of Wei, Wu Qi did make his way south to the State of Chu where Duke Dao did appoint him Prime Minister in 389 BC. He carried out all of the reforms in this book, as well as others. They changed the way the State of Chu operated and put it back into a powerful position. The nobles hated it, and they killed him for it.

Here are a few more interesting historical tidbits:

The State of Chu and the State of Yue met on the battlefield in 402 BC, but it wouldn't be until much later, in 334 BC, that the state was defeated by Chu outright.

Wu was a very common name. Besides Wu Qi and Wu Wei there is also the Wu River and cities named Wu. In fact, the State of Yue's capital was called Wu.

The Jiang River was the early name given to the Yangtze River. It was used by pre-imperial people and it wasn't until the 13th century that it got its current name. Poet Wen Tianxiang named it in his poem *Yangzi Jian* for the first time.

Dagger-axes were a very common weapon during the Warring States period. Infantry used the 9 to 18 foot weapon to kill, maim, and even unseat drivers from their chariots. It was really nothing more than a thrusting-type spear with a large blade attached to the top, a blade that was designed for beheading. Soldiers would thrust out their spear at the onrushing enemy and then, when the soldiers had jumped out of the way, they'd jerk the weapon backwards, pulling them in with the scythe-like blade.

There are no doubt a lot more fascinating things about the period, but many are lost to us. After all, the events in this book took place in the late 5th century BC, or nearly 2,500 years ago. It's much easer to recreate through a novel than it is to record through history.

I hope you've enjoyed Book 2 of the Warring States Series. Book 3, The State of Qin is available!

THE *STATE OF QIN* PREVIEW

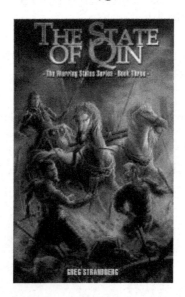

Wei Yang slowly worked the rag over the bristles of his brush, his eyes scanning up from time to time to the fat merchant standing on the other side of the table. He found one of the last remaining clean spots on the dirty rag and began working it in between the bristles, gently coaxing the ink off for another few moments. He then held it up before his face. His jaw worked from side to side as he studied the implement that had done so much for him over the years. Satisfied that it was as clean as it was like to be just now, he put it back into its spot among his other brushes and ink in the small black writing case at his side.

"I think you'll find that everything is in order," Wei said as he pushed the chair back and stood up from the table.

The merchant grunted, not taking his eyes from the thin parchment, eyes that were screwed up tightly and peering down at the paper as if there was some hidden meaning there. For the man most likely there was, Wei knew, for although he had assured Wei that he could read, writing being his problem, Wei had doubted how *well* he could read. Looking at the man now Wei wondered if he could at all.

"Ahem."

Wei's cough seemed to get the man's attention, for he took his eyes off the paper and looked up.

"Yes, I think this'll do just fine," the merchant said, his eyes on the paper once more. "You did include the bit about the amount owed if delivery isn't made on time?"

"It's right there at the top, under the amount owed," Wei replied coolly. He had already adjusted the document once based upon the merchants demands, and was then forced to start over completely when he'd had to adjust them yet again. A job that should've taken no more than an hour had taken three, and it was now well past dark. All Wei wanted was to collect his pay and find the nearest inn.

The man finally put the paper down on the table, folded his hands in front of him, and then looked up at Wei.

"Well, it was five *bu* that we agreed upon, wasn't it?" The man began fumbling about in a deep pocket of his robes.

"Five *bu* for a single document," Wei said quickly as the man still searched "You required three."

"Now, wait a minute," the merchant bellowed, his

search for the coins suddenly halted, "it was one document that I asked for, and one that you gave me."

"You have *three* documents, as you can plainly see," Wei said, motioning toward the two discarded papers lying on the far side of the desk. "One was nearly complete when you requested changes, changes that couldn't be made any other way than by starting over completely. Paper and ink aren't cheap, you know, and I can't simply dismiss their waste. One document you *requested*, but it was three you *required*."

The merchant pulled his hand from his pocket and reached for the other two documents, bringing them up close to his face.

"The one is nearly complete, and I'm sure that you can find a use for it, perhaps even having it recopied at a much cheaper price than what I charge," Wei said to placate the man.

The merchant put the two documents down on the table and looked up again at Wei. "I will pay you for two of the documents, then, ten *bu*. The other, as you yourself admit, is of no use to me."

"Three documents, fifteen *bu*," Wei said.

The merchant rose from the table, his massive bulk nearly blocking out the light of the few candles burning behind him, and reached into his pocket once again. This time he seemed to remember where his coins lay, for his hand was out again in seconds and flipping toward the table. Several spade-shaped coins fell and clattered along the tabletop, the shiny bronze glinting in the candlelight.

"You'll have ten," the merchant said gruffly, "and be thankful for that much. You may have been recommended as the best, but five *bu* for one paper is robbery."

Wei said nothing as he bent over the table and gathered together the ten coins, quickly putting them into a deep pocket of his robes. He'd heard the same from many merchants before and wasn't surprised to hear it again now. Most refused to pay anything over the initial five *bu* cost, even if numerous papers and pots of ink were required to meet their demands; Wei was slightly surprised this man had agreed to give him the extra amount.

"If you're ever in need of another document..."

"I won't be," the merchant cut-in quickly, his arm raised to show Wei toward the door.

Wei gave a slight smile, put his writing case under his arm, nodded, and made his way to the door. A servant was waiting in the long hallway and showed Wei to the front of the large residence that the merchant called home. The man opened and held the door for Wei, and all at once Wei was back out on the street, free once again to do what he liked, exactly as he had been for the past five years.

What he wanted to do at the moment was get a good meal and a warm bed. It was much colder now than when Wei had gone into the merchant's house several hours before. He pulled his robes tight and began walking toward the business district of the city, hoping that the long walk from the large residential area would at least warm him in the chill night.

After several minutes the large tree-lined streets, nearly empty of people this late in the evening, began to give way to the narrower and more-crowded sections of the city. The area made up of first floor shops and second-story homes for the vast majority of common citizens who called Yong home. It bustled with activity during the day, but at this time of night it was dead.

Wei glanced around at the small shops selling food, clothing, and other goods, and the myriad trade shops nestled in amongst them. They were small, family affairs mainly, and small in comparison to what he would find in the other states' capitals. But then Yong wasn't a typical capital; it was in the State of Qin. By far the weakest of the Seven States, Qin didn't even deserve to be considered as one of the Seven if you listened to most anyone who didn't call it home, and even a few who did.

But Qin was also a lot more than just the weakest. In the time that Wei had spent there during his years of traveling he'd come to recognize the state as being the poorest, the dirtiest, the smelliest, the most dangerous, and, even though it was not the most northern of the Seven, the coldest.

That cold was seeping into Wei despite the brisk pace he'd set for himself, and he pulled his robes even tighter. Despite not having spent much time in the city he knew the streets well enough, and a few more twists and turns down the larger avenue brought him to a small street and the destination he had been seeking, a small wooden sign swaying lightly in the chill breeze, a mug of ale and a brush etched into it.

The Tankard and Quill it was called, and attracted a more educated sort of clientele, certainly quieter than what would be found just a few streets over near the gates, and it was the only place that Wei stayed in when he was in the capital. He pulled the heavy wooden door open and was happy to feel the inside's warmth rush out at him. He stepped in and quickly pulled the door shut behind him, not wanting anymore of the cherished heat to escape. He made a brief scan of the room and selected an empty table against the wall and near the fire, and no sooner than he'd sat down than a serving woman was by his side.

"Tea, as hot as you can make it, and whatever it is you're serving for dinner tonight," Wei said to her as he settled his writing case on the table.

"Rice and vegetables is all we've got this late," the woman said as she set a cup and teapot down on the table. "Pork all ran out an hour ago."

"That'll be fine," Wei said as he looked up at her. "I hope the rooms haven't run out as well."

"No, we've plenty of those still. Will you be needing one?"

"I will," Wei replied with a smile.

The woman nodded, her face looking as if it hadn't changed expression in years, and walked back toward the kitchen.

Wei put his hands around the tea and grasped the cup tightly, happy for the warmth that it imparted to his cold hands. He blew onto it, the steam moving momentarily, and took a soothing sip. One thing that could be said for Qin at least, they still knew how to make a good cup of tea.

Keeping the cup nestled in his hands, Wei took a better look around the room. There were a few tables with only a single occupant like himself, each of the men busy writing. One table held three men in light-brown peasant robes, each eating their dinners of rice and vegetables, and perhaps even a sliver or two of pork. But it was the last two tables, four men seated at each, which quickly drew Wei's attention. Confucians, Wei could tell right off, and it wasn't so much because of their grey robes that so marked the adherents to that school of thought. Their loud and boisterous conversation was peppered with words that only a Confucian would throw about so often and with such force.

Honesty, loyalty, humanity, righteousness, integrity, and *filial piety*; Wei heard them all coming from the two tables, and in span of only a few minutes. Obviously the men were feeling good, the wine they were throwing back by the flagon no doubt helping; it certainly was putting them into the mood to pontificate. What might have begun as a discourse amongst themselves was now more of an impromptu and drunken speech directed at the entire establishment, even those that were trying to get some rest in the rooms above.

"A ruler must show humanity to his people, for it is the only way that the people will love him," one man said between sips of wine.

"But it is not solely the duty of the people to love him first," one of his companions quickly added, standing from the table. "Loyalty must first go to one's family, and then to one's spouse. Only then can it be directed toward one's ruler, and finally toward one's friends."

"And if the ruler does not show humanity then it is the duty of the people to withhold their loyalty," the first man declared proudly, throwing back the last of his wine to make his point.

"And for Shangdi to withhold the Mandate of Heaven," another man added.

"So true, so true," the first man said as he filled his cup once again. "And that is exactly what Su Xiong should realize. By instituting the Legalist reforms of the outcast general Wu Qi, Duke Dao brought down Shangdi's disfavor upon him and the State of Chu."

Wei couldn't take it anymore. "Could it not be argued that General Wu's reforms in fact lifted up the vast majority of the peasants and gave them a better life, one they never could have had if those reforms were not made?"

The man that was speaking halted his cup midway to his mouth and stared out into the room.

"Who said that?" he said, his eyes blearily scanning into the pall of smoke from the fire and kitchens.

"That one over there against the wall by himself," a man seated next to the drunken orator said, pointing toward Wei.

Why did I say that? Wei thought to himself as the man shambled out from the table and started toward him. *Why did I have to argue with a Confucian? It never amounts to anything but dry throats and headaches.*

"You there," the man said, who Wei was beginning to think of as the Orator. His wine was sloshing from his cup as he made his way toward Wei's table, staining the grey fringes of his robes. "What was that you said?"

"I said that perhaps the reforms in Chu did more for the people than you realize," Wei said, his eyes locked on his cup of tea.

"The reforms did..."

The Orator trailed off as a large smile came to his face and he turned around to face his companions.

"A Legalist, boys!" he shouted. "We've got a Legalist here among us tonight."

The man turned back to face Wei, a large smile on his face, and Wei turned his head up to face him, his face stony and cold.

"I came looking for a hot meal and a warm bed, not a discussion on principles, and certainly not an argument over whose school is right," Wei said firmly.

"Oh, did you hear that, boys?" the Orator shouted back over his shoulder. "He doesn't want a discussion, only a warm bed."

"Then why did he speak up?" another man said as he and a few others rose from the table and headed toward their companion and Wei.

Wei groaned inwardly, realizing that it was now going to be a long night. Confucians and Legalists had never gotten along, mainly because the two schools of thought were so diametrically opposed to one another. While Confucians prattled on and on about virtue and humanity and what the world should be like, Legalists actually turned words into actions, making changes that had real effects, effects which often angered Confucians, either because those plans often went against their own ideals or, most suspected, because they actually worked.

"I'll tell you why he spoke up," the Orator said, "because he's right and we're wrong." The man stared down at Wei with a mocking grin that turned Wei's stomach.

Unlike most Confucians, many of whom Wei had run into during his travels and talked at length with quite civilly, this man was bent on argument. Just the sight of him made Wei cringe, not from any fear, but from sheer revulsion. The man was nearly as large as the merchant that Wei had just finished working for, although the Orator's appearance wasn't anywhere near as lavish. His grey robes were stained up and down with wine, many of the stains looking to have been from previous nights in similar inns and taverns. His beard and mustache were thick and bushy and hairs sprouted every which way, while Wei could tell that his hair, even tied back in a long queue, was greasy and most likely hadn't had a proper washing in weeks. The man was in sore need of new clothes, a trim, and a bath, and his companions weren't much different.

"We simply view the world in different ways is all," Wei said loud enough for everyone in the common room to hear. "If you would like to discuss the finer points of our schools I would be more than happy to do so in the morning over a hot cup of tea and a bit of food."

"I'd much rather have that discussion now," the Orator shot back to hoots and cat-calls from his companions. "I've always found wine to aid in discussion much more than tea."

"Well that is one point that we differ on then, for I find that it only leads to arguments and sore heads come morning."

The man's smile slid from his face and he frowned down at Wei. "He's afraid, boys, that's what he is."

Wei shook his head. "No, but I am tired and hungry and would like nothing more to have a quick dinner and retire to my bed."

It was obvious that the Orator wasn't going to let that happen, however, for he moved even closer to Wei, blocking any escape from the table, and bent down, his sour breath caused by more than just wine.

"You'll not be running away so quickly, legalist," he

said, his companions crowding in behind him, their presence and shouts urging the large man on.

Wei wasn't simply going to be walking away from the table tonight. He craned his head up so that he could see around the large man. The whole of the common room was watching and waiting for whatever would happen, and judging from the expressions on most of their faces they didn't think the outcome would be good. The serving woman was standing near the bar, a plate of vegetables and rice steaming next to her. She didn't seem in any rush to deliver the meal that Wei knew was his. He couldn't blame her; bringing food into this escalating situation would most likely only mean more cleanup work for her later.

From out of the kitchens came a small, wiry man who spoke a few words to the serving woman. She turned her head to speak with him and nodded toward Wei. The man nodded, slipped out from behind the bar, and headed toward the front door.

"I said you'll not be running away," the Orator said again loudly, drawing Wei's eyes back to him.

"No, it appears not," Wei replied.

The man smiled and turned his head back to his companions.

"It seems we're already starting to put some sense into him boys, in another few–"

Whatever that 'few' might have been neither Wei nor the man's companions were to find out. When the Orator had turned his head back to his friends Wei had grasped onto his writing case with both hands. As the man started to turn his head back, Wei jumped up from his seat, swung the case with all of his might at the man's face, and connected right with his mouth, the impact breaking open the case to send brushes and inkpots flying every which way.

There was a loud crunch, so bad that even the Orator's companions groaned and winced at the sound, before the man fell backward into the men behind him. His companions they might have been, but Wei knew then that none were his friends. They simply let his body fall back toward them, not a one making a move stop his fall. The Orator landed with a thud onto the hard wooden floor. His hands grasped at his mouth in pain, and blood welled-up through his fingers.

The inn became deafly quiet after the Orator hit the floor, and it was all that anyone around the man could do but look down at him, waiting to see what his reaction would be. Wei knew what his reaction would be, for although the blow had been a strong one the Orator wasn't unconscious. Wei knew that when the shock of the blow ended the Orator would be back on his feet. Wei would do best to be well away by that time.

He sidled out from the table and began moving around the group of men that stared down at the large Confucian. Wei heard the Orator groan and spit out a glob of blood and a few teeth. But by then he was halfway to the door.

"Stop him!" a cry came from behind Wei.

Wei knew the man was getting back to his feet as soon as he heard the shout and he quickened his pace. The Orator's table was between him and the door. A few men that hadn't rose to cheer on their large friend were still sitting there, but at the shout they rose and blocked Wei's path.

"Where's your writing case now, Legalist?" one of the men taunted, but Wei feinted one way and went the other when the man was thrown off. The next man wasn't quite as gullible or drunk, and when Wei tried to get by him he grabbed onto Wei's robes and pulled him back.

"He's mine!" bellowed the man clutching Wei's clothes as he spun him about.

Just a few feet away the Orator was already back on his feet and coming toward Wei, blood streaming from his mouth. Wei looked around quickly but there was little at hand that could be used as a weapon. He gritted his teeth and waited for the beating that would come, hoping it wouldn't be the death of him.

"I'll kill you for that, Legalist!" the Orator yelled as he spat out more blood. Wei could see that several of the man's teeth were missing from the blow he'd received.

"That wouldn' be in line with your beliefs as a Confucian," Wei said in jest, although it was a true statement.

One of the Orator's companions laughed and nodded his head, but the Orator quickly silenced him with a look.

Wei was about to say something else, more placating, but the Orator didn't give him a chance. As he turned back to face Wei had threw his heavy arm out and punched Wei right in the gut, doubling him over. He would have fallen if the man clutching his robes had not held him up. Wei gasped for breath but the Orator wouldn' let him have any. He threw another punch into Wei's stomach and then one across his face, connecting right with his cheekbone. The pain shot through Wei and he must have blacked out for a moment, for he didn't remember hitting the floor. All he knew when he came to was that the man was standing over him, his bloody and toothless smile looking down as he readied another blow. Wei closed his eyes, expecting the worse.

"Halt!"

Wei's eyes flew back open at the shout and he saw that the man was no longer looking down at him but toward the door.

"City watch," one of the men huddled around Wei said quickly, and the group quickly dispersed as men rushed back toward the kitchens and whatever back door might be there.

Wei tried to turn his head around to see how many

of these city watchmen were coming into the inn, but his gaze instead became locked on the man's bloody smile once again. The Orator obviously wasn't going to let a few guards stop him from finishing what he'd started. Wei tried to huddle up into a ball as much as possible as the man's foot slammed into his stomach.

"Stop now!" another shout came from the approaching watchmen, but they weren't approaching fast enough. The Orator's boot slammed into Wei's stomach again, and then stomped down onto his face. Wei was expecting another blow and pulled his hands up to cover his head, but it never came. Slowly he opened one eye and then the other. Instead of a boot coming toward him he saw a watchman's hands reaching down for him and then pulling him up.

"You sure angered that one," the man said as he got Wei to his feet.

Wei looked at the man decked out in the red robes of the city watch and then down at the man on the floor. Blood was pooling from his lifeless body, staining his already wine-stained robes an even darker shade of red.

"You killed him," Wei said, not taking his eyes from the dead Confucian who only a moment before had been pummeling and kicking him to death.

"We told him to stop, twice," the guard replied. "Would you rather we waited until he'd finished with you?"

Wei's eyes went from the dead Confucian to the guard, but got caught halfway when he saw the bloody dagger-axe clutched in the man's hands.

"Can you walk?" the guard asked.

Wei felt his head spinning but nodded that he could. He stretched his leg out and took a step, then another. The guard let go of his robes and he tried to take another, but crashed down to the floor instead. He looked up at the guard as another man came to stand beside him.

"Will he live?" the new man asked, a man Wei recognized as one sitting at a table near him before the fight broke out.

The guard frowned and shook his head.

Wei tried to keep his eyes open but failed.

Check out *The State of Qin* today!

ABOUT THE AUTHOR

Greg Strandberg was born and raised in Helena, Montana, and graduated from the University of Montana in 2008 with a BA in History. He lived and worked in China following the collapse of the American economy. After five years he moved back to Montana where he now lives with his wife and young son. He's written more than 50 books.

www.bigskywords.com

Other Exciting Books
by
Greg Strandberg

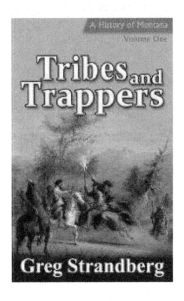

Montana history comes alive from the time of the dinosaurs all the way to 1840. Learn about Lewis and Clark and the various mountain men that came after them. Discover Montana in Tribes and Trappers!

It's been six months since the horrendous incident atop Mount Misery, the incident that broke Beldar Thunder Hammer's band of adventurers apart. Now Beldar's putting the band back together. Why? To head back up Mount Misery to end the Kingdom's Hireling system for good. A tale of epic fantasy adventure unfolds, one you won't want to miss!

1075 AD. William the Conqueror's army sits outside Norwich Castle, the siege of three months going nowhere fast. The men need ale, but there is none. One man can get it for them, Sir Peter Godfried. He sets out, and along the way he finds love, trouble, laughs, and a hideous plot to upend the kingdom in this humorous and edgy historical novella.

There's a secret underground alien base in New Mexico, one sanctioned by the federal government. But that base got away from the military in 1975. Now it's 1979 and time to take it back. Discover Dulce Base today!

Find Greg Strandberg's books on Amazon, Apple, Barnes & Noble, and other retailers

GREG STRANDBERG